Great Day in the Mornin'
Country Folks Cuttin' Up

by

G. P. Marrow

This is a work of fiction. Names, characters, places and incidents are the product of the author's imagination. Resemblance to any actual event, locals, organizations, or persons, living or dead, is/are entirely coincidental and beyond the intent of the author or publisher.

Mailing address

Black Deer Books
P. O. Box 841
Henderson, N C 27536

BLACKDEERBOOKS.COM

Copyright © 2010 by G. P. Marrow

All rights reserved. Except for use in any review, any and all parts of this book may not be reproduced in any form whatsoever (electronic, mechanical, xerography, photocopied, or in any type of informational storage retrieval system, developed or undeveloped at the time of this publication) without the written permission of the author, except as provided by the U.S. Copyright Law

ISBN 10: 0-9729455-5-5
ISBN 13: 978-0-972945554

Library of Congress Control Number: 2010916287
Printed in the USA

Ruth Russell – Williams

The print portrayed on the cover, 'Workin' Cotton', is one of many masterfully created works of art by the late, self-taught, world renowned folk artist, Ruth Russell-Williams.

Born, the child of sharecroppers in the tiny community of Williamsboro, North Carolina, many of Mrs. Russell-Williams' paintings draw upon her childhood on the farm, picking cotton, working alongside her grandmother as a domestic, and attending the family church.

Her artistic achievements are many and include such noteworthy accomplishments as a portrayal of her painting, 'Outdoor Baptism,' on the cover of The Smithsonian Magazine; receiving the key to the city of Cincinnati, Ohio; induction into the Sigma Gamma Rho National Hall of Fame; sales contracts with J. C. Penny, Burlington Coat Factory, Nordstrom, Roses International, and Michael's Department store.

Numerous newspaper and magazine articles have been written honoring Mrs. Russell-Williams' artistic talents, including *"The Artist As A Young Girl"* in the Raleigh News and Observer, *"Simply Beautiful"* the Durham Herald Sun newspaper, and the June, 1999, issue of Essence Magazine.

In 2003, she was included in the 23rd Edition of *Who's Who in America*, and *Who's Who among American Women*.

Her work, '*Forty Acres and a Mule*' was commissioned by author, Phyllis R. Dixon, for the cover of her book, '*Forty Acres*'.

In 2006, her work, '*Day Lillies*' was commissioned for use in a Mazda commercial, in 2008, she donated twelve works to the H. Leslie Perry Memorial Library, in Henderson, North Carolina, in 2005, was featured in North Carolina publication, '*Our State*' magazine, and profiled on WRAL TV's Tar Heel Traveler in 2009.

I give a very special thanks to Mrs. Russell-Williams' son, Cecil Russell, now president and CEO of Ruth Russell-Williams' Art Enterprises, for releasing this print for use as the cover of my book. We both agree that it ties in so appropriately with the contents of most of the stories included in this text.

ACKNOWLEDGMENTS

First of all, I give thanks to the Almighty for bestowing upon me this unique gift that has taught me how to finagle with the written word.

I'd like to thank my Sister-Friend, Mary Noble-Jones for her never-ending support and encouragement. And her loving husband, Bobby who always had my back.

I'd like to thank Anita Ballard-Jones for pushing me beyond the limit and rousing me into action to complete this book in the most professional delivery possible.

I must send a shout out to my number one supporter at Vance-Granville Community College, Ms. Helen Holt, whose encouragement helped to stimulate my desire to see this literary project to its fruition. And to my wonderful Creative Writing instructor, Mr. David Wyche, who taught me how to instill life into each character by giving them a speaking voice.

I would be remiss if I did not give thanks to the entire teaching staff of the former Kittrell Graded School, for their caring and professionalism in providing a first-rate education for me and every student who attended that esteemed institution, during the most impressionable years of our educational journey. They encouraged us to strive for our highest achievements. They did not allow us to cut corners or settle for anything less than our very best. They disciplined us with love and conviction and I retain the deepest respect for every teacher whose instructions I had the privilege of receiving.

I extend grateful acknowledgement to all of the friends and neighbors who lived on Peter Gill Road, and to those who were fellow classmates and schoolmates at Kittrell Graded School, for we were more than just fellow students, we were an extended family.

I offer special acknowledgement of those friends and neighbors in the tiny crossroads community of Gill, for the inspiration I found in their character and personality, which motivated me to create some of the characters in this book..

DEDICATION

This book is dedicated in loving memory of my dear mother, Martha Ann Carroll-Marrow, who instilled in me a profound love of the written word. May her memory, and that of my father, Walter Marrow, both of whom inspired the characters in two of the stories contained within this volume, live on in the stories and remembrances of our bitter-sweet existence as share-croppers on a tenant farm in rural Vance County, North Carolina.

I'd also like to dedicate this book in memory of my wonderful, young friend, Master Christopher Maurice Hawkins, who I loving called my 'twin.' And to my late sisters, Sarah, Gracie, and Lola Mae, may they all rest in eternal peace.

INTRODUCTION

"Great Day in the Mornin'." is a selection of short stories written over the past forty years. They are stories from childhood memories of growing up in rural Vance County, between Kittrell and Henderson, North Carolina. Some of the contents of each story are based on similar events, but seasoned with a hefty dose of fiction.

All of the characters in each story are fictitious; however their roles in the story may have been inspired by the individual temperaments of former childhood acquaintances. Their personality, intrigue, and sense of nature has compelled me to personify the unique traits and characteristics they demonstrated, as an inclusion in this book, as I attempt to bring those wonderful years of country living back to life.

Although the trials and tribulations of trying to exist as tenants on a sharecropper's farm were bitter-sweet at the very least, the ultimate goal of writing these stories, was to highlight more of the sweet and less of the bitter.

My sincere wish is that anyone who grew up on a tenant's farm will find a little bit of sweetness with which they can identify, within the contents of at least one of the situations described in this volume.

And may the stories in this book remind everyone who reads it, of the days when life was sweet, simple, full of possibilities and rich with the goodness of Mother Earth. A time when we not only neglected to lock our doors, but we rarely closed them until the chill of winter's breezes started creeping in.

A time when it was still safe to sleep on a home-made quilt with the family pet, on the front porch and enjoy the cool, summer breezes under the light of the moon, while listening to the sounds of nature singing the night away.

I hope that reading this book will put joy in your heart and a smile on your face, and inspire you to take your own personal trek down memory lane.

It's the next best thing to turning back the hands of time.

ENJOY and GOD BLESS!

TABLE OF CONTENTS

HAYRIDES	1
COTTON-PICKIN' SCOUNDRELS	6
MY FIRST DAY AT SCHOOL	18
SNUFF & CURIOSITY	31
GUNNY SACKIN'	41
THE DEVIL GOT A HOLD OF ME	41
TOSSIN' TOBACCO WORMS	61
RINGIN' A TEN	71
PITCHFORKS & BARE FEET	78
BLACK MARIA	85
HO DOWN SHOW DOWN	91
CAT RUN	102
SOUTHPAW SAM	113
THE SETTIN' UP	127

POETRY

GRE'T DAY 'N DE MORNIN'	146
GUNNY SACKIN'	148

ABOUT THE AUTHOR 151

HAYRIDES

This morning, for no special reason, Bo, Jimmy Lee, and Ralph hitched Ol' Red and Buck Shot to the wagon and rode down the road, picking up every stray kid in sight.

Cally, Joan, and me, were the first ones to thumb a ride, hanging on the sides of the wagon, broadcasting to the entire neighborhood that a hayride was underway. Bales of hay were stacked, one on top of the other, all the way to the rim of the wagon's railing.

Before the wagon reached that roller coaster dip we adoringly called Peter Gill Hill, the bales of hay were covered with twenty or more singing, clapping, and swaying country bumpkins.

When there were no more houses in sight, June Bug Davis pulled two, half-gallon Mason jars of Blackberry wine from under one of the bales of hay, and proceeded to pass it around and let everybody sample a taste of the dark red intoxicant.

Cally handed the jar to me and I pretended not to want any saying, "I ain't no drunk, so don't hand that nasty mess to me. Do y'all know how stupid you look after y'all drink that mess, falling all over the ground like a bunch of drunken skunks? Thank you, but, no thank you. Somebody on this wagon needs to keep a level head an' I intend for it to be me."

June Bug leans over and says to me, "Why don't you just admit you ain't got what it takes to handle this here Blackberry wine, gal!"

Now, June Bug knows full well that I can't stand to be called 'gal', especially by no guy, so I grab the jar out of his hand, turns it up to my mouth, and take a big gulp. It strangles the pure heck out of me. I let go of the jar, and Marshall catches it before it hits the hay. I grab my throat, gasping for breath. I cough and heave and spit 'til my throat is raw. June Bug is stretched out on the hay, laughing his head off.

I'm fighting mad. I kick him so hard with my right foot he rolls off the bale of hay and lands on Bo's back. The jolt causes Bo to lose his balance and jerk on the reins hard enough to make Ol' Red and Buck Shot rear up on their hind legs. They go into a full gallop. The wagon wheels start making zigzags in the gravel on the road. The straps break and Ol' Red and Buck Shot are on the run. Now the wagon is out of control. One of the wheels hit a dip in the road causing it to become airborne and flip on its side. We all go sailing through the air.

I landed on a huge patch of grass and ended up with a bloody nose and a mouth full of dirt. I rose up on my knees, spitting red dirt and blades of grass from my mouth. I glance over at the person next to me and notice that Jenny Cook has a bloody lip but seems okay otherwise.

Everybody jumps to their feet at the same time, asking, "Is everybody okay?"

We all answer, "Yea, I'm okay," as we brush the grass and dirt from our clothes. Marshall takes a handkerchief from his pocket and wipes the few drops of blood from my nose and Jenny's lip, as I continue trying to clear all of the dirt from my mouth.

"Y'all gon' be okay," Marshall says. "Just a few drops of blood, t'ain't that bad." Then he gives us both a strong hug.

We all grabbed a hold of the side of the wagon and heaved and pushed until it's upright again. The mules were nowhere to be seen. The last anyone saw of them both, they were going over the other side of the hill.

I sat back down, straddling the shallow ditch that separated the road from the pasture which ran parallel to it. I looked down and right beside me, lay a fully intact jar of unopened Blackberry wine. I picked it up, leaned over to June Bug, who was sitting on the other side of the ditch facing me, and say, "I don't know 'bout you, but I can sure use a drink," as I pass the jar over the ditch to him. He twists the top off and hands it back to me, saying, "Ladies first."

I take the bottle, turn it up to my mouth and take a big swig of the enticing elixir, that was surprisingly bitter and sweet at the same time, and let out a loud, "Ahh!," and hand it back to June Bug.

He takes an even bigger swig, and passes it on to the next person. We pass the jar around 'til there is nothing left in the bottom but dregs, and needless to say, by this time, we are all feeling no pain.

Bo stands up and staggers over to the wagon. He looks back at Marshall and June Bug and says, "Which one of y'all wanna play mule an' help pull this wagon back to the stable?"

Marshall staggers over to Bo and grabs a hold of the reins, speaking in a slurred voice, "I take the front. You take the back, an' we go rollin' 'long," as the three of them turn the wagon around back in the direction of the stable.

We all stumble to our feet, laughing and drooling like rabid animals, looking for a place to position ourselves along the sides and back of the wagon, to help push it back up the hill and two miles down the rocky road back to the stable.

About a mile from the stable, Marshall turns around, looks back and starts laughing. "Now if this ain't puttin' the cart 'fo the mule," he says.

I look back to see Ol' Red and Buck Shot casually following our lead, but keeping a safe distance, back to the stable. Everybody start laughing.

Jenny starts singing,

Ninety nine bottles of Blackberry wine
Ninety nine bottles of wine
The mules ran away
We spilled all the hay
Ninety nine bottles of Blackberry wine . . .

We continue our sobering trek, some pushing, some pulling the no-mules wagon back to its parking space, all the while continuing our silly jingle,
Ninety eight bottles of Blackberry wine
Ninety seven bottles of Blackberry wine . . .

. . . until we reach the stable, huffing and puffing. The two brainy, dignified mules stroll delightfully into the welcoming outbuilding and proudly position themselves over the feeding trough. They proceed to devour a hefty helping of freshly spread hay, with a self satisfying smirk on their faces.

I sheepishly glance over at June Bug, who says, "I do believe we just been outsmarted by two dumb mules. 'Cept I think we the dumb ones. Can you imagine just how stupid we must've looked, pushin' that wagon down the road wit' Buck Shot an' Ol' Red strollin' so careless behind us? I can hear the white folks now when they was lookin' out the window watching us dummies do the mule's work. 'Them lil culud chil'ren ain't 'xactly right, is they? They must be 'flicted or somethin'. Ain't nobody ever told 'em the mules s'posed to be the ones pullin' the wagon an' not them? Look like they folks coulda took the time to teach 'em a lil good, ol' fashioned horse sense. Po' lil, dumb, culud thangs.'."

We just fall out laughing at his mockery of those imagined on lookers. But the laugh really was on us drunken fools looking like a pack of country jackasses: First cousins to Buck Shot an' Ol' Red.

A late note:

Today, Peter Gill Hill no longer exists. It went to an untimely demise more than two decades ago. All that's left is an unassuming dip in the road.

Sometimes, when I venture off the beaten path, and cruise down Peter Gill Road, I press on the gas pedal when I reach that landmarked spot, and try to relive the thrill we felt when the car sped down the hill, bounced when it hit the bottom, and revved its engine to climb up the other side.

Unfortunately, the thrill went along with the hill, and the modest burrow that remains, is merely a bump in the road.

Some folks might say that losing a country landmark like Peter Gill Hill is the price you pay for progress.

I simply say, ***"BUMP THAT!"***

COTTON-PICKIN' SCOUNDRELS

    I often wondered whatever became of the Murphy twins who lived down the road from our house. The last I heard, they'd both been accepted at some college out in the Midwest, which explains why the area is constantly plagued by terrible storms and tornados.

    Those two, especially the one named Miami, are probably out west raising astronomical turbulence and stirring up all kinds of sadistic spirits.

    They were inseparable; thick as sorghum molasses. Their devilish little antics sometimes made me look like an angel. And that was no easy feat. They were my kind of people. They never ran out of annoyingly impish pranks to pull on somebody. I actually have to give them credit for some of the inspiration I gained from observing their rascally behavior.

    We were all around the same age. Miami, the oldest twin by two minutes and forty six seconds, practically dwarfed her sister, Minnie, who was nearly a half foot shorter than she. Both had faces so freckled, they appear to have a permanent case of chicken pox. Two fiery-red pigtails cascaded half way down their backs. And to say they were 'foul mouthed' was a definite understatement.

Miami was always the ring leader whenever they got into mischief and devilment. I always felt that Minnie went along with whatever mischievous scheme Miami concocted in her demonic little brain because she was intimidated by her sister's size and afraid of the consequences if she defied her wishes.

They used to set booby traps for the Thompson boys on the farm next to ours, even though they had huge crushes on both of them.

Rafe, who had jet black hair, eyes as blue as the ocean, and could charm the hair off a wooly ewe, and his younger brother, Daniel, with dirty blonde locks and crater-deep dimples, were country gentlemen in every sense of the word.

One day, Miami got the notion to put pine cones under the horses' saddles, after she saw the boys saddle up for a ride.

Out of nowhere, we hear a cry from behind the stable, "Help! Somebody help me."

We all ran behind the stable to see who it was. It was Minnie, sitting on the ground holding her left ankle. She looked up as the boys approach her. "God, it hurts," she cried. "I stepped in a hole and twisted my ankle. God it hurts like the devil."

Being the courteous young men that they were, the boys picked her up and carried her inside for their mom to look at her ankle.

Minnie hugged them both and ever so innocently said, "How can I thank y'all? I don't know how I woulda made it if y'all hadn't come to rescue me. Thank y'all ever so much."

The boys graciously said, "You welcome," and left the room.

I stood in the door, trying not to throw up my breakfast after witnessing Minnie's stellar performance, followed by her miraculous recovery.

Meanwhile, Minnie's distraction gave Miami time to place the pine cones under the saddles and find a good place to hide and watch the show.

Before the boys could climb up on the horses, Minnie had a ring-side seat on the back porch to witness the end result of yet, another of their rascally pranks.

As soon as Rafe and Daniel climbed up on the horses and the weight of their bodies pressed the saddles down on those pine cones, making them poke into the horses' flesh, they bucked them both off. And the two brothers ended up stretched out on the ground.

Miami and Minnie had themselves a good laugh.

I thought it was a terrible prank, but I had to laugh, too, because they never ran out of mean things to do to somebody, and each caper got more creative than the one before, and they **Do Not** discriminate. . .

I was walking pass the house one Sunday morning when I heard Grand Pa Henry cussing like a sailor. "Dangnappit! Who the devil put this pile of cow mess in front of these steps? I got crap all over my Sunday shoes. I can't go to church wit' my shoes smellin' like cow manure!"

Somebody had strategically placed a big, sloppy, maggot-infested blob of cow manure in front of the steps, knowing that Grand Pa Henry never looked down and would step in it.

"Grand Pa, Henry!" Miami called out, pretending to be shocked at the foul language spewing from his mouth. "You need to repent for cussin' like that on a Sunday. God gon' be mad at you."

"Don't you say nothin' to me 'bout foul language, you lil, sassy-mouth whippersnapper! I heard words come from yo' mouth that could stir up a tornado. And, b'sides, this here seems awfully like one of yo' stunts. So what you gotta say for yo'self, young lady?"

"T'won't me, Grand Pa Henry," she lied. "MaraBelle probably broke pasture ag'in and came past the porch. You know she craps everywhere she goes. I swear on the Good Book, t'won't me."

"Sure t'won't. And you kin sell me some swamp land in Alabama," he argued.

I tell you, the few occasions when I had the gumption to hang out with those dishonorable twins always taught me a thing, or two about devilment and deceit. I witnessed some wild stunts being pulled by those two cotton-pickin' scoundrels of the female persuasion, and some of them were downright disgusting.

One of the grossest things I ever saw them do was nurse MaraBelle, Grand Pa Henry's milk cow.

Sometimes we'd take a shortcut across the pasture, on the way to the pond. Before we left the house, Miami had asked Grand Pa Henry for a glass of milk. His response was, "You git some milk wit' yo' supper."

Miami didn't argue, and a diabolical expression came over her face. When we approached the stable, Miami asked me, "You ever drank milk from a cow?"

I answered, "Of course I do. Every day."

She said, "I mean really drank milk from a cow."

I firmly repeated, "Of course I do, you idiot. Every drop of milk I drink comes from a cow."

Then she shook her head to let me know that I was not getting the message and says, "Naw, you don't understand. I mean do you drank milk from a cow like this?" Then she got down on her knees, grabbed hold of one of MaraBelle's tits, and went to town sucking like a newborn calf.

The poor cow just stood there looking confused.

Then when Miami had sucked her belly full of milk, she looked up at Minnie and said, "Yo' turn."

Minnie obeyed and had herself a good drink of fresh cow's milk.

After Minnie was done, Miami looked at me and said, "Now it's yo' turn."

I turned around to see if someone was standing behind me because, surely, she was not talking to me, and responded, "Naw, it ain't! You two are the nastiest, most vile thangs I know. I ain't sucking on that cow's tit, 'specially after y'all had yo' germy mouths on it. You two are as disgusting as pure vomit. In fact, lookin' at the two of you makes me wanna do just that."

The truth is I just didn't wanna suck on that cow's tit. Then I pretended I was gagging and said, "You two are just po', nasty, uncivilized, backwoods heathens. You girls gotta raise yo' standards if you gon' keep hanging 'round wit' me. I have a reputation to keep you know. I can't be seen goin' 'roun' wit' no lowdown, half-raised mess like the two of y'all."

When I started to walk away, Miami mumbled, "Whatevah!"

I waved back at them and said, "I gotta go. See y'all later."

I swear 'fo cheese! There seemed to be no end to the creatively juvenile behavior of those two Murphy twins. Everything they did was criminal.

Sometimes, during the late summer, we might miss a day out of school and pick cotton to make some pocket money. Miami usually goofed off most of the time and had picked only two full sacks of cotton by the time they brought the scales around to weigh each person's pickings for the day. I happened to look up one time and spotted her heading to the end of the row. I saw her bend down and went to find out what she was up to that time. I was just appalled at what I saw.

"What in God's name are you doing?" I asked, when she straddled the open burlap sack, half filled with cotton.

"What it look like?" she snapped.

"It looks like you 'bout to pee in that sack of cotton," I snapped back.

"Well, then," she offered a counter response, "I guess that's what I'm gonna do." And that's just what she did.

I couldn't believe my eyes, so I asked, "What you do that for?"

"'Cause wet cotton weighs more, stupid," she answered.

"Who you calling stupid, you country heathen. I wouldn't think of doin' some of the wild stuff you do. And you the one who's stupid if you don't think they gon' notice that cotton sack is soaking wet."

"They ain't gon' see the wet sack, dummy. The wet cotton gon' be mixed in wit' the other cotton in the sheet 'fo it's weighed. You oughta try it sometimes."

"Not me," I argued. "I'm a lot mo' decent than you. I prefer to earn my money the honest way."

"Suit yo'self," she answered. "You so naïve."

Being the relentless juvenile that she was, she came back with, "Or if you don't wanna pee in it, then put rocks in the sheet when it's half full of cotton, to make it weigh mo'. Either way works just fine, and at the end of the day, you git paid for picking mo' cotton than you really did."

I gave up because I knew I was fighting a losing battle.

Each stunt those two evil twins pulled appeared more sinister and daring. Like sneaking into Grand Pa Henry's root cellar to sample some of that grape wine he made for church Communion.

I would just go along for the ride because Miami triple-dog dared me and called me a fuzzy-haired chicken. Then, too, I needed proof that she wasn't lying when she bragged that she stumbled up on the stash one day while trespassing in territory that was strictly off limits to us kids.

I knew the door to the root cellar was always locked so I wanted to know just how she gained entry into such a forbidden space.

As usual, Miami had an answer for every question. She claimed, "I accidentally see'd Grand Pa Henry hiding the key to the root cellar in a shoebox under his bed."

I asked, "What in the daylights was you doing poking 'roun' yo' Grand Pa's room?"

Her answer was swift, spontaneous, and nowhere near the truth. "I accidentally came by his door and t'won't shut tight, and I accidentally see'd him puttin' the key in the shoebox and slide it under the bed."

"That's a mouth full of crap," I yelled. "You must think I'm some kinda dumb idiot to fall for such a bald-faced lie."

"Well," she argued back, "I think you're a fuzzy-haired chicken and just makin' excuses 'cause you too scared to go down there."

"I ain't scared of nothin'. I just don't believe you know where the key to Grand Pa Henry's root cellar is, that's all."

"Then prove it," she dared me. "Prove you ain't scared to go down there. I triple-dog dare you."

At that moment she'd crossed the line and called my bluff. I had no choice but to go down there then.

She dared me to follow her into the root cellar. T'won't no way I could have no white kid calling me a fuzzy-haired nothing. That was an insult to my race and my curious nature, so I boldly march down the steps to the root cellar just as tough as you please. Talk about spooky. Before I knew it, I was spitting out all sorts of profanity. "What the S*%#t?! Y'all done brought me to the back side of Hades! Where the dickens is Saint Lucifer? This place is spookier than the graveyard. In fact, this place makes that crypt at Cedar Grove Cemetery feel like Ms. Molly Jones' tea parlor." Looking up at the ceiling I swore out, "Them the thickest cob webs I've ever seen hanging from that ceiling." I looked down at the floor and say, "This here ain't even a real floor. It's just packed-down dirt. And it stinks to high heck down here. No wonder Grand Pa Henry don't want nobody coming down here. This looks like a place folks come to be embalmed after they die."

The floor felt slimy under my bare feet when I stepped down on it. It was so damp and slick I lost my balance and almost fell. "Doggone, Miami," I beefed. "This place smells funky. It's damp, and a person could slip and break their neck on this slick floor. I don't think Grand Pa Henry gotta worry 'bout nobody coming down here messing wit' his wine, if there **IS** any down here. And don't you dare close that dag-gone door and shut out all the light. And I don't care if you do call me a fuzzy-haired chicken. This place gives me the pure creeps. I bet ghosts and all kinds of spooks be down here tap dancing 'cross this floor. If that door slams shut, I'm gon' crap bricks all over this confounded floor. This here just the kinda place some slick, country farmer like Grand Pa Henry would hide a stash of homemade wine, which I ain't seen one bottle of. So I ask you ag'in, where's the wine, Miami? Show me the wine! Or ain't there none? All I see is a whole lotta shelves going from the floor all the way up to the ceiling, and there ain't nothing on them but a whole lotta jars of canned food." I look down and continue, "You even got white taters an' sweet taters, spread out on the floor, so I repeat, where the devil is the wine Miami?"

Miami didn't say a word. She just strolled to the back of the root cellar and slid her right hand into a small crack in the wall, and let out a loud grunt. Right before my eyes an entire wall rolled open exposing another wall with shelves, from the floor to the ceiling. Every shelf was filled from one end to the other, from top to bottom, with bottles of Grand Pa Henry's vintage wine.

I was in countrified awe. My mouth fell to my chest. Miami had just exposed the mother lode of homemade Muscadine wine. Every bottle had a label that read 'for church Communion only.'

I looked at Miami and before I know it, I yelled out, "I be danged! We done struck gold. I ain't never seen so many bottles of wine in my whole life. Dangit, Miami, how long Grand Pa Henry been making this stuff?"

"Long as I can remember." she answered.

Miami retrieved a tin cup from her jumper pocket and held it up into the air, pretending to preach a sermon, "In the name of my Grand Pa Henry, bless this here wine and this day, and the hands that picked the grapes to make this wine. May it taste as good as it looks. Bless the chillun that's here, Lawd Henry, and let us git drunk as skunks so that we won't feel that paddle you gon' be using to tan our hides if we happen to git caught down here in this root cellar. And forgive us our trespasses. Amen!"

Minnie and I echoed, "Amen." Then we all fell out laughing and Miami popped open one of the bottles of wine and we started our childish Communion.

Miami poured a generous shot of wine into the cup, extended it out to Minnie and me, let out a loud "CHEERS," and turned the cup up to her mouth until it was empty.

She poured another good shot of wine into the cup and handed it to me.

I imitated her actions and extended the cup out to her and Minnie and offered an even louder, "CHEERS," and turned the cup up to my mouth until it was empty.

Next it was Minnie's turn and she repeated the ritual a third time.

We passed the cup around a few times until the wine bottle was more than half empty. Then reality sat in. Minnie started to panic. "Lawd, hammercy! How we gon' explain to Grand Pa Henry why this wine bottle is half empty?"

"Yea, Miss. Know-It-All," I repeat Minnie's question. "How we gon' explain to Grand Pa Henry why this bottle is more'n half empty? Huh?
Tell me that, Miss. Know-It-All."

Miami paused for a moment. Then a devilish smile came over her face. I could hardly wait to hear what kind of brilliant scheme she'd dreamt up this time.

She placed her right pointer finger on her cheek and says, "Oomh! You know," she chuckled with a devious glimmer in her eyes, "Somethin' liquid an' real wet."

"Like what?," I wanted to know. "You see anythang liquid and real wet that we can fill a half empty wine bottle wit'?"

"Well . . . naw, not yet," she answered with way too much confidence for comfort. Then she squatted down and peed in the cup until it ran over. The next thing I knew, she was pouring the pee into the wine bottle until it ran over. She wedged the cork back into the top of the bottle, wiped the bottle clean with the hem of her dress, and placed it back on the shelf as if it had never been moved. She pinched off a tiny piece of the lower left corner of the label and turned the bottle slightly to her left so that Grand Pa Henry wouldn't notice it the next time he came into the root cellar. And we'd recognize the bottle and won't drink from it again on our next trip. Nobody, but the three of us and God, would ever be the wiser.

I stood frozen in my tracks, in shock, with my mouth wide open, taken aback at the gall and sheer genius of that young, fiendish brain.

Suddenly Miami was my heroine. I had to admire the criminal brilliance of such a conniving act of deception.

We all staggered back to the house and Miami quietly put the key back into the box under Grand Pa Henry's bed, and the three of us come out looking as innocent as lambs.

We trampled out to our play house and stretched out on some burlap sheets. The next thing we knew, Grand Pa Henry was calling us to come to supper.

I walked with the girls to the back door and we said our good-byes.

Grand Pa Henry came back to the door. "Ain't you stayin' for supper, Prudence?" he yelled out."You more'n welcome. We got plenty."

"Naw. Thank you, Grand Pa Henry. I better be gittin' on home. See you later."

"See you later. Come back soon, okay."

"Yes, sir, I will."

Now, I must admit, Grand Pa Henry could cook some good smelling food, but he won't 'bout to talk me into having any of it. He'd let way too much chewing tobacco spit drop out of his mouth. And I won't exactly sure where it dropped. I won't about to eat no food that had been seasoned with chewing tobacco spit. So whenever he invited me for a meal, I just made up some excuse why I couldn't stay. That way, I didn't hurt his feelings, and I didn't walk home gagging from the thought that I'd just eaten food spiced up with tobacco flavoring.

The next time me and the twins sneaked into the root cellar and half emptied another bottle of wine, I got to fill the bottle back up with my pee. And the time after that was Minnie's turn.

We kept it up until we half emptied, and refilled, near half of those wine bottles with our pee, each time, turning the labels to the left, after tearing off a small piece of it, so that we could keep up with the ones we'd half emptied and refilled with urine.

A few Sundays later, after church, Miami, Minnie, and I met down at Wilson's Creek, where we'd sit and skeet rocks across the water.

Miami and Minnie started laughing.

"What's so funny?" I asked.

"We had Communion at church today," Miami informed me.

"What's so funny 'bout that?" I wanted to know.

"You know they have Communion every fourth Sunday and pass 'round them lil cups of wine. Everybody in the whole congregation took a big sip of wine as the Deacons passed the tray from one person to the next. Each and every person at church had a sip, 'cept me and Minnie, of course," she chuckled deviously.

"And why not?" I ask.

"Well, I recognized the bottle. T'was one of the bottles we refilled wit' pee.

"You right sure?" I questioned.

"Yea, I'm sure t'was 'cause I noticed a corner of the label was tore off."

"And what did they have to say 'bout that holy wine?" I wanted to know.

"Well, all they talked 'bout later on at the church social was how, in Miss. Molly Jones' words, exceptionally tasty that batch of wine was."

The three of us looked at each other and fell out laughing.

After that day, whenever the three of us got together, we'd have ourselves a good laugh about the Communion of the holy pee wine.

I raise my hand before the good Lord! If them Murphy twins weren't two female Lucifers, themselves, they surely were his first cousins.

Like I said, they were my kind of people: scum of the earth, mean as two gut-shot grizzlies, cunning as Wylie Coyote, and gross as a buzzard eating maggots.

What can I say, except, I learned the art of devilment and deceit from two of the best. And as ornery, and sly, and gross as they could be at times, in my opinion, they didn't come any better.

It so happens, they turned out pretty good. Word is, they both became nuns and manage a home for orphaned and abused children in Salt Lake City, Utah. Now is that ironic or what? Two former she-devils doing the Lord's work. I wonder if Hell will freeze over next?

Anyway, wherever they are today, I say, "Hats off to those sick, demented, and grossly despicable Murphy twins.

MIAMI and MINNIE, I HUMBLY SALUTE YOU!"

MY FIRST DAY AT SCHOOL
(Simply the Best)

Carterville Primary School, in Carterville, North Carolina, was my first, and to this day, remains the best educational experience of my life. Mr. Carter, the principal, and all of the teaching staff at Carterville Primary School, created an atmosphere that extended far beyond the normal boundaries of most elementary institutions of learning.

We were a family, and Mr. Carter and the staff took an active role of becoming, not only educators, but guardians, counselors, caretakers, mentors, and even friends.

They turned what could have been the most traumatic day of my young life, into one of new discoveries and life-changing events that have helped to charter the course of what may have been an uncaring, unassuming life, into one with an insatiable appetite for learning.

I view every day of my life as a learning experience, and I have the teaching staff at Carterville Primary School to thank for the awesome revelation that I will never become too old to learn something new.

Back in the late 1950's, when I entered the first grade, that was my introduction to the world of public education, because there was no such thing as kindergarten, pre-k, or Head Start in this area. That was also the day I had to sever that invisible umbilical cord that kept me perpetually attached to my mother's apron string.

She was the scope of my world; lock, stock, and barrel. A forced separation from her was like being submerged in icy cold water without thermal swimwear to keep me warm, or an air tank to help me breathe.

Most children would be overjoyed with excitement at the prospect of attending school for the first time. Huh, not me. I didn't believe a word of all that garbage I'd been told about meeting new kids, making new friends, learning new things, discovering a whole new world through books.

I was convinced, beyond a shadow of a doubt, that it was just a plot to get rid of me. I would lie in bed, imagining the teachers all had fangs like Dracula, warts like frogs, and probably ate little children for breakfast.

The principal, Mr. Charles Carter, was as big as Paul Bunyan, without the axe and flannel shirt. I felt like someone being condemned to nine years of hard labor. That's how many years I'd be confined to that anticipated evil death hole.

I had not slept one minute all night long. I'd heard every last tick of that clock beside my bed. All I could do was count down the minutes before I went to face the devil, because I figured it would be nothing less than pure torture.

Everybody I knew from the first to the ninth grade, kept telling me to try and get in Mrs. Sawyers room because she was so sweet. I didn't care how sweet she was. If I never met her, I'd be just fine.

Ma had been preparing me for my first day at school ever since the last school year had ended early last June. All I heard was how much fun I was gonna have. And my mind always had the same response, *then, you go. I can live without it.*

To make things worse, Ma had enlisted my half-brained cousin, Judy Mae Green, to escort me to my designated room. There went what little hope I had left. How could my mother put the life of her baby child in the hands of a person who was dumb enough to put her finger in the light bulb socket to see if the lamp was plugged into the outlet? And, I tell you no lie, that's just what that cockeyed moron did.

One day I went to visit the family and found Judy Mae sitting in the dark, just twiddling her thumbs, moving her eyes from side to side like she was waiting for something to happen. I asked her what was going on and she said, "The lamp won't come on."

Being the sensible person that I was, I asked, "Is the bulb blown?"

She just shrugged her shoulders and said, "I don't know," and kept twiddling her thumbs.

Knowing her mind was too slow to address more than one question at a time, I walked over, pointed to the table, and suggested, "Why don't you see if the lamp is plugged into the outlet?"

Now, I knew better, so I can only assume that I must have experienced a moment of temporary amnesia to make such a deadly mistake.

She stood up, reached over and unscrewed the bulb from the lamp, laid it on the table, and plunged her hand down into the empty hole that the bulb had occupied.

I had looked down for a moment, but quickly raised my head upon hearing the crackling sound coming from the lamp. Every strand of Judy Mae's shoulder-length pony tail stood to itself. She looked like a black version of Sparkle Plenty from the old Dick Tracy comic strip. Her eyes threatened to pop out of their sockets, and drool was running down the sides of her mouth. I was not about to touch her while she stood there doing a freakish rendition of the shimmy. But I knew I had to do something before the fool died of electric shock, so I grabbed the broom and used the handle to yank the cord from the outlet. She fell back in the chair.

Now, a half normal human being would have suffered permanent damage to the brain or some other part of the body. But since Judy Mae had very little mentality to spare, the Lord was merciful and let her snap back to her normal self. And I use the word, 'normal', loosely.

Ever since that day, whenever Judy Mae combed her hair in the dark, sparks shot out in all directions, like sun rays. It was a hard pill to swallow knowing that my mama ignored her own sense of foresight and entrusted my safety to a person with such a limited amount of mental capacity. But that's just what she did.

The day before I was to enter the first grade, Ma did everything in her power to create a little enthusiasm in me. None of it worked. She had me try on the new dress she'd lovingly made for me with the embroidered collar and sleeve edging. That didn't do a thing for my temperament. She even washed my hair as usual in rain water, combed it out neatly, and pressed it out to the straightest style that I can ever recall. Then she brushed my hair into the cutest ponytail, made me a perfect bang twisted up on brown paper and tied into a knot. After which, she tied it all up in a cotton scarf to be removed the next morning before I left for school.

Then that doggoned rooster, Ol' Crow Eyes, started crowing like there was no tomorrow. I glanced over at the clock and saw that it was 3:38 A. M. I got up, went outside and grabbed the biggest rock I could find, hurled it through the air, and knocked his lights out. On the way back inside, I yelled out, "Guess you'll shut up now, you big mouth, fuzzy head Cock-A-Doo-Doo." One hour later, that rascal was at it again. I swore, "Dog gone it, I thought I killed that rascal."

Daybreak finally arrived and Ma opened the door to peek and see if I was awake. I pretend to be sleep. A few seconds later she shook me, "Git up Portia. Time to git dressed for yo' first day of school. Ain't you excited?"

I said under my breath, "Heck, naw! I'd rather have that confounded Chicken Pox ag'in!"

Ma went back into the kitchen. I followed her. She made my favorite breakfast, pancakes and eggs, puts them on the plate, sat it on the table in front of me, and said, "Go 'head, baby. Eat yo' breakfast while t'is still hot."

In the meantime, she went about her business fixing a bag lunch for my first day at school . . . a bologna sandwich, five peanut butter crackers, and a flawless red apple. While I was still sitting, she placed a shiny, new nickel on the table for me to purchase a carton of milk in the cafeteria to wash it all down with.

My stomach was so full of butterflies, I couldn't even swallow, so I just retreated to the room I shared with my sister and waited for the prison guard, cousin, Judy Mae, to come and escort me up the path to the bus, and to my homeroom, when we get to school.

I knew the knock on the door was Judy Mae, but I didn't say a word. She called out, "Portia, t'is me, Judy Mae. I come to walk you to the bus. You ready?"

I sat on the bed thinking to myself, *I just can't believe Ma gon' trust me all the way to school and back wit' this dummy? This should be interesting.*

I got tired of her relentless knocking, so I got up and opened the door.

"You ready for yo' first day at school, Portia?" the dummy asked.

I stared her straight in the eyes and said, "Heck, naw. Is you ready for it?" Then I brushed past her and ran to the kitchen and grabbed hold of Ma's apron, begging, "Please, Ma, don't make me go. They gon' kill me an' boil me in a big pot of vinegar an' water, an' serve me up for lunch. I hear tell they all eat dark meat there like wit' people from the jungle. If you send me to that place, you ain't gon' ever see me like this ag'in. The next time you lay eyes on me, I'm gon' be comin' out somebody's doo-doo hole."

Ma had to laugh, but didn't say a word. She just took me by the hand, led me through the house to the front door, put my hand in Judy Mae's hand, and went back to the kitchen.

Half way up the path, I started putting on brakes. Poor Judy Mae huffed and puffed, trying to get me to the road before the bus stopped so the driver wouldn't have to wait for us.

I started begging again. "Please, cousin. If you make me git on that bus, you gon' have to live wit' the guilt of my death on yo' hands for the rest of yo' life. An', if they don't boil me an' serve me for lunch, I'll be so messed up for the rest of my young, precious life, they'll have to take me to the crazy house at Camp Butner an' git paid twenty five dollars to let 'em experiment on my brain. You don't want that on yo' conscience, now, do you?"

Judy Mae was so dumb; I thought I had her for a second. Then, all of a sudden her brain decided to kick in, because she turned around and said, "You just joshin' me, ain't you, Portia? You had me goin' there for a minute. I been 'ttendin' this school for eight years now, ain't nobody ate me up."

All I could think was, *Yea. You been goin' there for eight years, but you just in the fifth grade, what does that say about you, big dufus dummy. And, besides, who the devil would wanna gnaw on yo' mangy hide? Buzzards wouldn't eat you if you was the last bone at a Fourth of July Bar-b-q.* But I just left it alone, knowing I was talking to somebody whose brain never caught up with the rest of her body.

Judy Mae kept tugging and I kept resisting. But since she stood close to six feet tall, at the age of thirteen, could cut and haul more wood than the average man, her muscles were a lot stronger than mine, and she managed to hoist me into bus, #28. The driver promptly closed the door and pulled off.

I swore and punched her the entire eleven miles from our house to Carterville Primary School.

As the bus arrived at the school yard, I saw two other buses, #44 and #10, unloading kids in front of the breezeway. When our bus pulled up, I opened the emergency door and tried to escape. Judy Mae was not only stronger than the average man, she was also just as fast. Before I could stretch my legs far enough to jump out of the back door, she stretched out her super long arm, grabbed hold of my blouse and said, "I done just 'bout had 'nough of you. If you don't stop actin' like a spoiled cousin, I'm gon' tan yo' hide so bad, you won't sit down for a week!"

I retaliated saying, "An' if you even try it, I'll beat the cow-walkin' snot outa you, an' pull every bit of that red, kinky hair outta yo' scalp, you nappy-headed pimp ninny!"

At that moment, she swung me around back towards the front of the bus and practically dragged me up the aisle and down the steps to the ground. I tried to break away again, but that heffa had a death hold on me, and all my attempts to escape were in vain.

She gripped my left arm so tight, it started to go numb, as we climbed the three steps from the ground to the breezeway. We turned right and went through double doors and then made an immediate left. There were classrooms on both sides of the hallway. The two first grade classes were at the very end of the hall. Mrs. Sawyer's room was the last one on the left. I stayed to the left side of the hall unaware that we'd end up at her room. When Judy Mae and I started to enter the room, Mrs. Sawyer met us at the door.

Judy Mae said, "You got a new student, Mrs. Sawyer. This here's my cousin. She just startin' school today."

Mrs. Sawyer said, "I'm so sorry, girls. My room is full." She turned to Judy Mae. "You'll have to take her to Miss Bevin's class 'cross the hall."

My little heart sank to the floor. Then I was really mad. When Judy Mae started across the hall, I resisted more than ever.

"I ain't goin' to that evil voodoo class. Miss Bevin gon' put a root on me and turn me into a toad frog. They said I could be in Mrs. Sawyer's room.

See, y'all just a bunch of big, fat liars. An' you, you big, dumb, scatter-brained %$#@* witch wit' a 'B'. I hope the devil comes and gits you and take you home an' fry you in a pan of hot lard like cat fish." I continued to curse her, and gave her a swift kick to the ankle.

She grabbed my shoulders and put a hold on me so tight, I couldn't move a muscle. She literally carried me across the hall to Miss Bevin's room and slammed me down in a chair in the back of the room, which was really the front of the room since it was right in front of the door, and Miss Bevin's desk was in the rear of the room.

Miss Bevin, a thin, light-skinned woman, wearing dark-rimmed, cat-eye glasses, got up and came to greet us. Judy Mae told her she was my cousin and that I was just starting school that day. Miss Bevin reached out to shake my hand. I looked towards the window and totally ignored her. Then she looked at Judy Mae and said, "You can go on to yo' own class so you won't be late. We'll be just fine."

Judy Mae headed for the door, but stopped just short of reaching the hallway, looked back and said, "Hope you can have a good day, cousin."

I mumbled under my breath, "An' I hope you can kiss my foot, you big ox," just as she turned to head down the hall.

Miss Bevin turned around and said to the rest of the class, "Class say 'hello' to yo' new classmate. What is yo' name, sweetie?" she asked.

I gave no response what so ever.

Miss Bevin told the rest of the class to introduce themselves. One child after another stood up and proudly announced their identity.

"My name is Bobby Johnson."

"My name is Rena Reavis."

"My name is Herbert Royster."

Every child in the class introduced themselves, except me.

Miss Bevin bent down and said, "If you don't tell us yo' name, we won't know what to call you. So can you please tell me yo' name?"

I had become permanently deaf and dumb, and refused to open my mouth. I figured if I behave badly enough, this could easily be my first and last day in this place, because Miss Bevin would become so fed up with me, she'd send a note home, telling Ma to never send me back.

Boy was I wrong. The next thing I knew, poor Miss Bevin was going through the entire alphabet, calling out names, hoping I'd respond to one of them. She started with the letter A. "Is yo' name Alice?' I offered no response. "Is yo' name Brenda, or Beulah, or Betty?" Still no response.

"How about Carol, or Christine, or Cally?" I refused to mumble a word.

"Well, maybe it's Delores, or Debra, or Daisy?" My lips were sealed tight as Fort Knox.

That charade went on for at least half an hour.

Finally she got to the P's and asked, "Is yo' name Phyllis? Or Paula? Or maybe Portia?" I nodded my head. She let out a huge sigh of relief. Then she turned to the rest of the class and instructed them to, "Say 'hello' to yo' new classmate, Portia McCoy." Everybody said, "Hey, Portia," in unison. I offered no response, but wondered, *what makes her think she knows my last name?* Then it came to me, *she figured 'cause Judy Mae an' me are cousins, then we must have the same last name.* **WRONG!**

When the class took a bathroom break, I refused to go, and was left in the class alone, but Miss Bevin was close by.

Five minutes after the class returned, I got up and started to leave the room. Miss Bevin called out, asking, "Where you goin', Portia?" I returned to being a deaf mute.

She rushed down the aisle and took hold of my arm. "You can't wander the halls alone Portia, so please take yo' seat."

I just stood there for a few minutes, then a brilliant idea came into my devious, little head. I remembered my scheme that if I behaved badly enough, I probably wouldn't have to ever come back again, so I grabbed the trash can and ran into the hall. I pulled down my bloomers, peed in the trash can, pulled my bloomers back up, returned the can to its original spot, and sat back down. Miss Bevin was in shock, staring at me with her mouth wide open. No one but Miss Bevin and I were aware of the prank I'd just pulled. Her next action caused me to think to myself, *this woman must be crazy,* because, instead of being mad at me, she broke out into a hysterical laugh. In fact, she laughed so hard, she bent over and whispered in my ear, "I'm 'bout to pee in my pants. I may have to use that trash can myself." Then we both had a good laugh.

The rest of the class just stared at us in confusion.

Before I knew it, it was time to go to lunch. Miss Bevin had been at the blackboard teaching us the A, B C's, when she looked up at the big, white-faced clock on the wall and said, "Okay, children, put down your pencils and line up to go to the bathroom an' wash yo' hands for lunch." We followed orders as she lead us to the door, turned around, and said, "Portia, you get behind me." I reached under my desk and retrieved my lunch bag on the way to door.

We went to the bathroom, washed our hands, and made our way across the breezeway to the cafeteria. The aroma of home-made cooking filled the air. I grabbed a tray and lead the class through the lunch line. Mrs. Terry and Mrs. Waddell, the two cooks, piled up everybody's plates, except mine and eight other children's, with fried chicken, string beans and potatoes, steamed cabbage, chocolate cake, and baked corn bread, that smelled so good, it almost made my mouth water. I gave Mrs. Terry the nickel and she placed a small carton of milk on the tray beside my lunch bag.

By the time we finished filling our bellies at the lunch table, we were all too full to even think about learning anything, so Miss. Bevin lead us outside for recess. On the way there, she took us into the band room and let us choose a toy to exercise with. Since I thought I was the queen of swing, I chose the Hula Hoop.

We followed Miss. Bevin down the hill to the biggest playground I ever did see. I turned around in a full circle and said, "Wow, this bigger than the fairgrounds wit'out the Ferris wheel."

When Miss. Bevin instructed us to stop, I stepped over into the middle of the Hula Hoop, pulled it up to my waist, and circled my hips from side to side, showing off my Hula Hooping skills.

Bobby Jones, Nathan Pierce, Hubert Hicks, and Walt Thompson, started playing dodge ball. Within minutes, I see Nathan grab hold of his left ear and go running to Miss Bevin, wailing like a big baby, after it got slammed with the ball.

Miss. Bevin gave Nathan a consoling hug, all the while, giving Bobby, Hubert, and Walt a good lecture about playground safety. "You boys know better. That's a very hard ball. T'won't meant to be thrown at someone's head. The first day of school an' I have to send a child home wit' a headache. What do you have to say for yourselves? Oh, never mind. Line up," she ordered. "Recess is over."

We all fell in line and marched like little soldiers, back into the classroom. Miss. Bevin instructed us to, "Take out paper and pencil and lets pick up where we left off wit' our A, B, C's."

We took turns going to the blackboard to trace the dots she'd made in the shape of the alphabets. Then she handed a pile of paper to Temple Rainey, with the same outlines and told her to, "Pass these out to the class so they can practice at their seat."

Just when I was really getting into the classroom activities, the three o'clock bell rang. Time to go home. I survived my first day at school, and went home thinking, *that place ain't so bad after all.* Once I realized just how much I had to learn about human nature, I appreciated that my little stunts had failed miserably. Miss Bevin didn't buy one bit of my amateur antics, but made me aware that day was the beginning of the rest, and best of my life.

When I arrived home, Ma had a big glass of cold milk and a plate of freshly baked, still warm, and very chewy tea cakes waiting for me. I dove in without hesitation.

The next morning, I was the first person to hit the floor, anxiously looking forward to that bus ride to Carterville Primary School. I didn't even wait for Judy Mae to come for me. I met her at the bus stop and barely escape being hit by the door, I was so eager to get on board. Judy Mae couldn't figure out where all my enthusiasm was coming from. And I couldn't imagine volunteering to tell her that I'd actually come to like the place in only one day, without any persuasion from her. She actually believed her little threat to, 'tan my hide', scared me into behaving better. What a joke. And it's gonna be even more funny when my report cards end up at her house, since my last name is not McCoy.

Before I knew it, six weeks had come and gone. Report cards came out for the end of the first grading period of the school year. Miss Bevin promptly placed mine in Judy Mae's hand when she came for me at the end of the day. She passed it on to me when I stepped off the bus at the end of our path. I rushed through the door to show off my good grades. Ma never even noticed that the wrong last name was written on the envelope. McCoy and not Macon. All she saw were all of those 'S's beside every subject on the report card, which she proudly signed without hesitation.

The nine years I spent at Carterville Primary School opened the door to a world that spanned the globe through books and a dedicated staff of teachers and a principal who we lovingly called 'pop.'

During the course of those nine years, the world witnessed the first piloted space flight. America mourned the assassination of our 35th president. The Vietnam War began during my tenure at Carterville Primary School. And Dr. King made his world-wide, historic, "I Have A Dream," speech on Capitol Hill.

To say that the years I spent at Carterville Primary School were nine years of constant red-letter days would be an understatement, to say the very least. They were, in my opinion, the best learned days of my life.

They say it takes a village to raise and nurture a child. Well, Carterville Primary School was the proverbial African village. They not only taught us our A, B, C's and 1, 2, 3,'s, but also a love for the entire learning process. We learned discipline with love and assurance, and acquired enormous respect and adoration for real professionals who went the extra mile in every class they taught. All to guarantee us a better life than the ones they had experienced. And I have to say they pulled it off with flying colors.

In my humble opinion, the education that I received at Carterville Primary School was "Simply the Best."

A note of praise and gratitude to the principal and teaching staff of the former Kittrell Graded School, my inspiration for writing this story of fiction, exclusively for the entertainment of the reader.

Hats off to 'Pop' Paschall, Ms. Wright, Ms. Hatton, Ms. Brame, Ms. Best, Mr. Pointer, Ms. Marable, Ms. Massenburg, Mr. Thomas, Mr. Allen, Ms. Mitchell, Ms. Manley, Ms. Rowland, Ms. Dixon, Ms. Balthorpe, Ms. Spencer, Ms. Branch, Ms. Cheek, and any person whose name I omitted from lack of memory. Thank you all from the bottom of my heart. May those of you who have passed on to the next life continue to rest in eternal peace.

"I extend deep love and admiration to each and every one of you!"

SNUFF & CURIOSITY
(Hanging Out With Mrs. Vidalia Dawson)

When I was a youngster growing up on Peter Gill Road, in the early and mid sixties, my bestest friend in the whole, wide world, was an elderly lady I lovingly called, Mrs. Vie. She was already in her late sixties and I was at the tender age of nine, and literally her human shadow. I trailed behind Mrs. Vie everywhere she went. I'd spend the better part of some days, especially in the summertime, at her house, watching her fill those old galvanized tin wash tubs with hot water she'd boiled on that old wood stove, and scrub clothes on a washboard all day long. Then she'd rinse each piece as it was cleaned to her satisfaction, wring it out with her weather-beaten hands, and hang them out on the line across the yard to dry.

I'd sit in their tiny kitchen observing her clean, batter, and fry the most delectable, crispy, golden brown chicken, pond fish, and pork chops I ever did see. Then I'd gladly help her and her husband, Mr. Bolger Dawson, eat it all up.

She'd bake home-made, buttermilk biscuits that rose an inch high. Then, for a tasty snack, she'd drizzle Grandma's Black Strap Molasses on a plate and I'd sop that plate clean, with two or three of those fluffy biscuits.

Mrs. Vie and her husband, lived in a tiny, unpainted, three-room, wood-framed house down the road from us. It had a little living room, a long, narrow kitchen, one small room upstairs, and no electricity. Their only source of light came from an assorted collection of oil lanterns positioned throughout the house.

I never ventured farther than half way up those enclosed stairs more than once, that I can recall. The steps creaked with every landing of my feet which made it more than a little too spooky to proceed beyond the halfway point. The bulk of my time there was spent either in the kitchen, or with my legs spread across the small, army type cot that rested against the outer wall of the staircase in the living room watching her sew or mend a pair of Mr. Bolger's socks, or replace a button on one of his flannel shirts.

I thought Mrs. Vie was one of the smartest people I knew. Although she'd had no formal schooling that I was aware of, the wisdom she possessed from sheer life experiences could have filled volumes.

I don't know if she and Mr. Bolger ever went to a real doctor in their entire lives. She had her own home remedies for everything from bee stings to diarrhea. And she loved to 'dip' snuff; Tupelo was her brand. She'd sit in that old rocker in the living room, with the palm-sized can of snuff in her apron pocket, and an empty fruit or soup can beside her to spit in.

She not only used it to satisfy her nicotine cravings, but for medicinal purposes as well. A hefty ball of snuff, saturated with spit, was a soothing balm for scrapes, minor cuts, or insect bites, just to name a few of its uses.

She would break a tiny stem from the Forsythia bush on the side of the house, and chew on one end until it was shaped into a fan. (I later found out that was an old custom passed down through the generations form our African ancestors.) After she had chewed the stick until it was perfectly flat, she used it to spoon the snuff out of the can, put a big scoop in her lower lip, and sit back to enjoy the seemingly calming effects of the dusty tobacco product that made me sneeze if I got too close to the open can.

Mrs. Vie had such a peaceful expression on her face when she sat in her chair rocking and sewing and humming a tune, most of which I did not recognize; all with her lip packed full of her powdery-brown habit. It was like her well deserved reward for all of the chores and hard work she'd performed throughout the day.

Sometimes Mrs. Vie would doze off while rocking, and dipping, and sewing in that squeaky, old chair and I'd stretch out on that cot and do the same.

Ma never worried about where I was when I'd be missing all day, especially during those summer months. She figured I was somewhere trailing behind Mrs. Vie, and she'd eventually see the two of us making our way up that dusty dirt road to our house.

Mrs. Vie was terrified of thunder storms. So, at the first streak of lightning or that initial roar of thunder, I expected to see her ambling up the road to ride out the storm at our place. Most times I'd meet her half way because I knew she'd never stay at home during a storm, even if she had to leave Mr. Bolger behind, because he refused to join her.

After the storm had blown over, I'd walk Mrs. Vie back home and visit for a while before returning home; sometimes looking forward to the next storm just to have a visit from her.

Mrs. Vie was only the second black female I'd known to wear a short 'natural' or afro in those days. Her little crop of hair was probably less than an inch long. Every week, usually on Wednesday, she'd come up to our house and either sit in a chair in the yard, where I'd stand behind her, or sit on a step of the front porch, where I'd sit on the next step up behind her, and plait about a hundred little interlocking sections of hair on her head. I'd neatly part each tiny division in a straight row, dip my right pointer into the can of Royal

Crown hair dressing, she'd brought along in her apron pocket, and gently rub a thin coating of the dressing on her scalp. Then I'd comb it all through and isolate one small section after another until her hair was plaited from one side to the other. The entire process took more than two hours. When I was done, she'd give me a shiny, new dime. I thought she'd given me the U. S. Mint. I would stretch that dime from here into the next county. So when she increased my hair-dressing salary to a quarter, I knew I was 'Colored Rich.'

The first time I saw Mrs. Vie create her brand of home-made lye soap, I thought it was the nastiest concoction I had ever seen. Just watching her add all the elements was enough to make you want to gag. First she started a roaring fire under one of the big iron pots that she boiled her clothes in on wash day. She filled it half way with water. Then she started throwing in the ingredients: large chunks of pork fat, left over pork grease, even pieces of bones that had meat still attached to them. And finally, the last and most important item, a bag of red devil lye was dumped into the pot. She let the mixture slowly boil for nearly two hours while constantly stirring it with a stick. After about ninety minutes, she dipped the stick into the pot, and rolled the mix around it. If the mixture took hold of the stick, it was ready to be removed from the heat, and the left over bones were scooped out and thrown away. After that, she poured the thick, hot liquid that looked like runny creamed potatoes, into pans about a half inch deep, and set it out to harden. Once the form was set into a solid piece of soap, it was sliced into 2x3 inch bars, wrapped in individual pieces of brown paper, and put up in a cool, dry place until needed. And she used it to clean everything from floors, to laundry, to the whole body from head to toe.

Being the curious child that I was, I asked, "Ms Vie, why did you throw the bones and all into the pot with the meat still on them?"

Her answer was so simple it almost made me feel stupid. "Lye will eat up anything," she said. "It'll eat meat right off the bones. That's why when I make the soap, I be sure to pour the lye in the pot real slow so it won't splash on me and eat the meat right off my bones." We both had to laugh.

Sometimes we would go on little nature trips deep into the woods and Mrs. Vie would dig up different kinds of roots, bring them back home, wash and boil them to make a big pot of tea. Sometimes the tea, depending on the type of roots, was used for medicine to treat certain ailments. And sometimes, it was drank cold, just for the pure refreshment. Like the Saffron tea she made by boiling the root, that looked like the tail of a turnip. We'd trample through the woods until we came to a thicket of brush that resembled the Azalea bush. Mrs. Vie would use her garden trowel to dig up the roots, haul them back to the house, and clean them thoroughly with warm water. After they boiled for about ten minutes, she'd discard the roots and let the tea sit to cool off and later on we'd sit back and enjoy a tall glass of tea with hot, ham-biscuits. Now, that was a treat.

Mr. Bolger was even more resourceful than Mrs. Vie because he basically taught her everything she knew. The first time I heard him say, "Vie, I'm gon' go down by the creek an' check on my 'rabbit gum'," curiosity would not let me resist the urge to ask what it was. So I dove in with both feet. "Mr. Bolger, what's a 'rabbit gum'," I asked.

He was all too happy to indulge my curious nature and invited me to go with him to see what it was first hand. I jumped at the chance and followed him into the forest with Mrs. Vie in tow behind me.

When we reached the creek, I saw a primitive trap shaped like a rectangle, lying horizontally on the ground. It was a simply structure made of twigs tied together with twine, and a trapped door that had been tripped by the rabbit confined inside. The box measured about twenty inches in length, maybe ten inches wide, and stood about eight inches high. A simple, but very effective method of hunting ingenuity.

I had to turn my head when Mr. Mr. Bolger removed the rabbit from the box, beheaded, skinned, gutted and washed him in the creek before toting him by the hind legs back to the house. During the night, Mrs. Vie had cut the rabbit into pieces like chicken, soaked it in salt water to get the gamey taste out, and the next evening, served it up with a pan of onion gravy and biscuits for supper. Talk about some good eating.

That rabbit and gravy still came in a close second to the frog legs we'd go gigging for on some moon-lit nights. We went at night because the frogs would see us coming in the daytime and hop away. At night, it was a different story. Mr. Bolger, Mrs. Vie, and I would all go trudging down to that same creek, each of us carrying a lantern in hand to blind the frogs with the light and cause them to freeze in their tracks, which left them vulnerable to whatever weapon was used for the slaying.

After Mr. Bolger had gathered as many frogs as he could, he'd bring them home and clean them for the next day's supper. Since the back legs were the only edible parts, every bite of the delectable, creek-food delight was savored.

Of all the quality time Mrs. Vie and I spent together, I think reading the classics to her was my overall favorite. She'd lay back in that rocker, close her eyes, and absorb every word I read. Sometimes I'd give her a little oral quiz just to see if she'd really been listening to me, before I'd start the next book. I'd ask her questions like, "What was 'Moby Dick,' by Herman Melville about?"

She'd raise her head proudly and say, "T'was 'bout the capt'n named Ahab who battled wit' the big, white whale." And I'd praise her for that succinct summary of the book.

Or I might ask, "What was, 'Uncle Tom's Cabin' by Harriet Beecher Stowe, about?" And she'd respond, "That one was 'bout how bad them po' culud slaves was treated back there on them plantations." And I'd praise her again and say, "Good job, Mrs. Vie. Ready for the next book?" And her answer was always an eager, "Yes!" And I would begin with the appropriate title.

"The name of this book is 'Poems On Various Subjects, Religious And Moral,' by Phillis Wheatley. This book is very special because she was the very first Black American to publish a book. And one of the few lucky slaves who could read and write because she was bought by a kind couple who treated her like family. She was kidnapped from her country, named Senegal, in West Africa, when she was just seven years old, and brought to America and sold on the slave market in Boston. Because she was educated, she wrote real pretty poetry and published a book in 1773. The poem I'm gonna read is titled, 'On Being Brought From Africa To America.' It goes like this,

'T'was mercy brought me from my pagan land

Taught my be-knighted soul to understand' . . ."

The more I visited Mrs. Vie and Mr. Bolger, the more free I felt to roam throughout the house at leisure. One day, totally ignoring all the other sticky situations I'd allowed my overly inquisitive nature to get me into, I stupidly decided to try a dip of that Tupelo snuff that she seemed to enjoy so much.

She was out back hanging clothes on the line, so I just helped myself to a good sampling of the cocoa-tinted powder and packed my lower lip with as much snuff as it could hold. Sixty seconds later every inanimate object in the room started moving. The chair started rocking so violently I thought it would flip over backwards. Those spooky stairs turned into an escalator moving at warp speed. I felt that old, worn out hoop rug slipping and sliding under my feet.

As usual, whenever I wondered off and found myself up to my neck in trouble, I retreated to my place of sanctuary. Home.

I staggered across the room, opened the screen door, and dragged myself down the three steps and out to the road, which was less than fifty feet from the front porch. I struggled to keep my balance on the planks that straddled the shallow ditch at the edge of the lane.

Halfway to the house, which was less than a tenth of a mile away, my legs became so heavy they felt like lead, and trying to keep my footing on those hefty gravels, was like wading through a knee-deep river of torrent waves.

I finally made it to that steep foot path we'd created, just short of the curved hill in front of our house, which was thickly over grown with thousands of wild, red, pink, and white roses.

Even when I was totally sober, it took some effort to scale that slippery uphill, red clay path. Most of the time, I had to grab hold of every weed or blade of grass, on either side of the path, just to make it to the top. So, needless to say, in my present, snuff-intoxicated state, I was having more than a little trouble getting even halfway to the top.

I made a half dozen futile attempts to crawl up the hill on my hands and knees, but each time, I only got half way, before I slid back down on my belly, and landed flat on my butt. For the life of me, I can't recall how I managed to wander into that patch of roses, but before I knew what hit me, I was waging a fierce battle against ten thousand prickly rose thorns. And the thorns were winning, hands down. By the time I found my way out of that thorny maze, my arms and legs were covered with endless red welts.

I managed to stagger past the outside of the dining room and ended up between those two Forsythia bushes, where I nearly puked my guts out. The foul taste that the snuff left in my mouth, made me heave even more, but there was nothing left to come up.

The well was only about a hundred feet away so I tottered over to it, took the dipper that was hanging on the side, dipped it into the tin bucket dangling over the top, that luckily, had been left full of water. And, Lord, was I glad. I barely had enough strength to crawl over to the well. I surely wasn't steady enough to pull a ten pound bucket full of water from the bottom of that forty-foot deep reservoir.

I sat down on the foot high concrete foundation, which supported the well, and slurped as much water as I could hold, into my mouth, to flush out the dregs of snuff still left in my bottom lip. I took another dipper full and poured it over my head to try and slap some sense into myself. It didn't work.

I sat on that slab of concrete for so long, too dizzy to stand up, that I ended up falling asleep. When I woke up, after God only knows how long, my chin was literally lying on my chest, and my hands hung limp between my open legs. Brown drool had saturated the entire front of my sleeveless jumper. I must have looked like the town drunk. And if I didn't look it, I surely felt like it.

The aroma of dinner simmering on that wood stove was tossed into the air as it found its way through the opened kitchen windows. But I had no stomach for supper that night. The mere thought of food made me start heaving all over again.

When I finally drummed up enough nerve to go through the back porch and into the kitchen where Ma was, she just glanced down at my welted arm and legs, shook her head, and went back to cooking. I had already put on my innocent-as-a-lamb face to try and soften her up, in case I couldn't come up with a good lie trying to explain this latest series of battle scars. But she never said a word. She had long since become accustomed to seeing me wear the occasional cut, scrape, or bruise, so to her, these were just the most recent in a long succession of minor scuffling injuries.

She never bothered to ask what had happened, or where I'd been, or what or whom I'd tangled with. I don't think she really wanted to know.

I always thought Ma had some sort of sixth sense anyway, and that she knew exactly what I'd done every time I pulled one of my dumb blunders, and therefore, she didn't need to ask. She already knew the answer, so she saw no use in forcing me to make up a bald-faced lie, trying to talk my way out of hot water one more time.

Every once in a while when I'd come home wearing one or two combat tattoos, she'd just look at me, wearing a smirk, chuckle softly, and go back to doing whatever it was she'd been doing before I entered the room.

Since I was not quite stupid enough to try and find out just how many details she actually knew about my rambunctious escapades in and about Peter Gill Road, I simply left well enough alone.

I don't suppose I have to actually come out and say it, but I never, ever again let curiosity get the better of me and attempt to take another dip of snuff of any brand. Madame Tupelo was a close encounter that snuffed the curiosity right out of this 'curious cat.'

Mrs. Vie remained none the wiser about my curious mishap with her habit-relished routine for the remainder of her life. And her supply of Tupelo snuff remained non-threatened in my company from then on.

The next time I got the notion to take a dip in or of anything, it was in that irrigation pond in back of our house. I dove in, went under a few times, and came up soaking wet, but I came up still sober and still in possession of most of my senses.

GUNNY SACKIN'
(Steptoe, Black Angus and Me)

Cousin, Steptoe and me woke up this mornin' hungry as buzzards in a bone yard. All night long I dreamed 'bout some roasted corn and black-eyed-peas.

Now, Pappy already brung in all his corn for the market, and me and Steptoe didn't have nary dime to buy one ear of corn with after priming tobacco all summer long. But that didn't make us no never mind 'cause we know just half mile down the road, on Three Toes Jones' farm is the biggest, greenest, field of corn this side of Coon Holler.

All we gotta do is grab ourself a gunny sack, throw it over our backs, and march, just as big as you please, right into that corn field on ol' Three Toe's place, and help our self to all the sweet, Silver Queen Corn we can eat.

It be so sweet, you can eat it raw. Why, it prêt near melt in your mouth. I can taste it already.

Now most, one hundred and sixty pound, twelve year old, red headed, colored boys can be pretty gutsy, but, Steptoe, he be a big, ol' scaredy cat. I always gotta talk him into everything. But me, I ain't scared of nothing. Not even the devil hisself.

Folks 'round here say I'm just as mean as the devil. But I just call it having fun. Usually at somebody else's expense. But what the heck, there's a lil devil in every thirteen year old, red-blooded American male. I just got more than my share.

Before you can say, "Lick Skillet," Steptoe and me had done put on our dungarees and T-shirt, and head to the hay loft to get our cotton sacks where we usually stash them 'til we need them.

In a blink, I toss them sacks down to Steptoe, slide back down that ladder, and we on the other side of Three Toe's irrigation pond so fast our head be spinning.

Now come the tricky part, sneaking through that pasture without that red-eye breeding bull of Three Toe seeing us. He is one mean ton of meat. He can't stand younguns ('cause me and Steptoe like to do target practice on his backside with rocks and spit balls), and he hates the color red something awful. You don't dare wear no red nowhere near that pasture, or he'll chase you faster than you can slap a tick off a hound dawg.

No fence can hold that devil when he's mad enough to see the color red. He'll walk right through that barbed wire like it was paper. I swear! The color red turns that bull into some kind of mad cow. And what you suppose Steptoe is dumb enough to wear today of all days? That's right, the brightest, red T-shirt he could find.

I look over at him and say, "You just askin' for trouble, or did you forgit that red-eye devil goes crazy when he sees the culuh red?"

He pays me no never mind at all.

Steptoe and me get down and crawl on our bellies 'til we clear that fence, and take off running like two convicts done broke off the chain gang. We run until we get on the other side of the pasture. Then we just slide under the other end of that barbed wire and shoot into that corn field like two bats outta Hades.

We clean out half a row of that corn field. I say to Steptoe, "We stay close to the middle. That way, it be hard to see us."

We fill them sacks like it was no tomorrow. That corn smells so good we gotta shuck a few ears right then and there. We eat like pigs . . . sometimes swallowing silk and all. Pretty soon I'm so full, I gotta sit and rest a spell.

Then we finish filling our gunny sacks to the very brim. It feels like mine weighs a ton when I throw it over my back. We both huff and puff 'til we make it back to the fence. We drag them sacks to the very edge of that barbed wire and sit down to check the whereabouts of that bull. I spot him way up at the other end of the pasture, scratching hisself on the side of the stable.

"We in the clear," I tell Steptoe. "He so preoccupied wit' scratchin' his backside, he'n gon' pay us no nevah mind."

We throw them sacks over the fence and slide under that barbed wire. We peep to see if that bull heard them sacks hit the ground. He didn't hear a thing . . . least that's what we think.

We get hardly ten feet across that pasture before that bull sees us and charges like a freight train. Me and Steptoe throw them sacks on the ground and run for heck fire and high water.

I look back and think, *how the devil kin somethin' that big run that fast?*

He's closing in on us too fast. I looked back again and see smoke coming from his nose when he lowers his head to pick up speed. I shift into overdrive, but ain't no way we gon' out run that rascal. I headed for that old oak tree near the feeding trough. Steptoe says, "Let's lay down an' play dead." I have to remind that ig'nant fool that, "You lays down an' plays dead when you's bein' chased by a grizzly bear. This here ain't no grizzly bear. This here's 2,000 pounds of pure, ragin' bull." And he agrees.

I don't know which one of us hit the tree first, but we both reach the top at the same time.

That old bull gets mad as heck 'cause he didn't get to trample our hides. He stomps his hoof into the ground and snorts like something gon' stark raving mad. He even rams that tree two or three times with his horns. Then he just stands there, swinging his head from side to side. He's so mad he raises his hind leg and pee all over that tree.

Me and Steptoe just sit up in the tree, watching that bull tear into them sacks of corn and eat until his belly is full.

Half the day done gone by and we still sitting up in the tree. That bull don't move more than twenty feet the whole morning. Me and Steptoe don't move not a' inch.

Now I'm starting to fidget on the limb. I gotta crap something awful. All that raw corn done tore my stomach up in a mighty bad way. But I ain't climbing down the tree to crap on the ground. No Sirree, Bob.

I try to hang my butt over the edge of the limb and let the crap drop down on the ground, but I keep losing my balance, and have to slide back up against the trunk of the tree.

Something in the tree makes me sneeze and all heck breaks loose. I crap all over myself. It comes all out the top of my dungarees and shoots half way up my back. It gets all over my T-shirt. It stinks so bad, I pull off my shirt and drop it on the ground. That bull runs over and starts stomping on it. Then he picks it up with his horns and tosses it into the air. It comes down and lands right on top of his head. He shakes his head, back an' forth, until the shirt falls on the ground. The next thing I know, that bull takes off running like a possum bein' chased by a coon dog. And he don't stop 'til he's inside that stable.

Me and Steptoe jump down outta the tree and run for all we worth. We get to the other side of that pasture and don't waste no time sliding under the barbed wire.

"We home free, now," Steptoe says. "Like the dickens, we is," I argue, crap running down my legs, puddling on top of my bare feet. "What Ma gon' say when I come home smellin' like a skunk?"

"That is some stinkin' crap you done," Steptoe teases. "You smell like somethin' just crawled inside you an' died. Jump in the pond an' let it wash out in the water. Aunt Mable just think you been for a long swim."

Sounds like a good idea to me, so I jump in, pants and all. And sure enough, all that crap comes out in the water.

After I'm done dirtying up the water in the pond, me and Steptoe just mosey on up the hill to the house as innocent as you please.

By the time we done romping around, my dungarees be good and dry, but still smelling like a pile of doo-doo.

I ain't got no intention of being nowhere close by when wash day comes around. So I just change my clothes and stick the stinking dungarees way down in the bottom of the dirty clothes bag, and let them rest up against the inside wall of the back porch. Ma will be none the wiser. Ain't no need in getting her all upset, trying to explain why the back porch smells like something the buzzards dragged in, so I just decide to leave well enough alone.

Ma always says, "The mo' you stirs crap, the mo' it stinks!"

When I turn and head for the back door, Steptoe pats me on the back and whispers, "See you later, Walt. I betta be gittin' on back home. Ma be lookin' for me directly. I sure enjoyed the sleepover."

Steptoe leaves the back porch through the screen door. I walk through the back door into the kitchen, and notice a wonderful, familiar aroma. A smell I'd recognize anywhere. I look at Ma and ask, "Is that what I think t'is?" Ma smiles and says, "Yes, t'is, son. Yo' favorite. Fried corn wit' hot biscuits an' black-eye-peas on the side. That kind Mr. Jones come by an' dropped off two baskets full of fresh vegetables he picked from his garden this mornin'. Brought us 'nough, taters, maters, squash, okra, an' corn to last us a week. Hope you good an' hungry?"

"Yes, Ma'am, I sure is."

I go over to the side table to wash my hands. Guilt was running through my veins like that soapy water was running between my fingers each time I dipped them into the bottom of the wash pan. We didn't have to sneak over to ol' Three Toes farm and steal his corn after all. And serve us right that bull got to eat it all. I thank the Lawd, the sight of that scrumptious food on my plate made that guilty feeling disappear just as fast it came.

Ma tells me "Go 'head, sit down, an' say the blessings."

I do as she says, sit down at the table, look up toward Heaven, and says, "I thank You, Lawd. I thank You for this food that I'm 'bout to receive. I thank You for the corn an' peas and these soft, fluffy biscuits, yes indeed. An' forgive me for all my trespasses. You know what I mean." I wink, still looking up at the ceiling, then continue, "Problem solved, Lawd. Amen!"

THE DEVIL GOT A HOLD OF ME
(Better Late Than Never)

The three o'clock bell finally rang. I'd been fidgeting at my desk for more than an hour, looking forward to my weekly visit to Big Ma's house. Ever since my mama died, more than a year before, I'd become more and more fond of and devoted to Big Ma, my mama's Ma.

As I exited the gate at the edge of the playground, a voice called out to me.

"Hey, you. You tryin' to git left or somethin'?" that handsome, new, dark haired bus driver, Paul Thompson, asked. "If you don't wanna walk all the way to Carroll Town, you better git yo'self over here, fast."

"I ain't ridin' the bus today," I informed him. "Go ahead."

Back then, once a week, on Wednesdays, I would walk three miles to my Grandma's house, rather than take the bus to Carter Elementary, five miles away, where it connects with another bus that drops me off in front of our big, two-story, white, wood framed house, at Route 1, Box 40-C, on Phillip Parker Road.

My best friend, Valerie Jackson, dressed in a white long-sleeved blouse, black and white checkered skirt, and black and white lace up saddle shoes, walked along with me to the corner of Pickett Farm Road; where she lived. Her long, black pigtails swung from side to side across her back like a pendulum with each step she made.

"If you take the path behind Fred Royster's store, you'll save yo'self 'bout thirty minutes of walkin'," Val informed me.

"I ain't never been through that path before," I said. "I'm scared I might git lost."

"Don't worry!" Val reassured me. "T'ain't no way you can git lost. The path leads right to the corner of Garner Road. When you git to that corner, there'll be a big rock that looks like it got no reason to be there. Now all you gotta do is remember the direction to yo' Gramma's house, which should be to the right. Then you home free."

"You right sure 'bout that?" I asked "I don't wanna git lost in them woods. Lawd only knows where or what they might lead to. I'm way too young to git eat up by some big, ugly, fat-lip, one-eyed Booka-Man."

Val laughed out loud. "You much too bitter," she teased. "Not to mention too tough. He'd have to boil you for more'n a week just to tender you up 'nough to keep from chokin' on yo' tough hide."

She laughed even harder, then continued, "You sho' is a big bag of hominy grits. Where you s'pose we gon' find ourself a culud booka-man? They all rides horses wit' white hoods on they heads. Girl, you crazy as a bed bug," she added, shaking her head. "A Booka-Man! I swear! I done heard it all. If you all that scared, just go round way of the road. It might take a lil longer, but then, you know what they said, 'better late than never."

She laughed once more, then turned down Pickett Farm Road and disappeared around the corner.

I stood at the intersection, hesitating. "Ahh, what the heck?" I say out loud. "I can't git lost in no woods. I'm a country Negro." I giggled, then continued. "We right at home surrounded by all these trees. You couldn't lose one of us in the woods if you tried."

I ducked through the back of Fred Royster's mercantile. The path was narrow and rocky. Soon, it intersects with another, wider path. I wasn't sure whether to go right or left because I couldn't remember how far Val said I should go before I saw the big rock. I didn't know if that **was** an intersection. It was just two dirt paths coming together. I thought for a minute then decided *I'll go left.*

As I inched along the path continued to widen. If a person had a mind to, they could have driven a small car or truck right through there, like on any other country lane.

It had been more than an hour since Val and I parted at the crossroad. The forest became more and more dense. Clouds began to form overhead. The sun slowly sank into the western sky, while the familiar night sounds of the forest began to stir; the crickets where chirping, frogs croaking and the owls hooting.

The autumn air stirred, causing the trees to sway, sending hundreds of red and golden-yellow leaves sailing through the air. The wind was chilling, getting more fiercer by the minute. My thin wind breaker was no match for the sudden gust of winds that came up this time of the year.

I figured I'd better find shelter."

I looked around and I knew one thing for sure, I was pretty good and lost. The path curled deeper and deeper into the woods. I cursed Val with every step I made, because it was her fault I was in that mess, and I couldn't wait to see her and give her a good, old fashioned, countrified piece of my mind.

The wind started stirring up such a dust storm, I had to stretch my eyes to the limit just to see fifty feet ahead of me. There, at the edge of the path, stood a tiny, run down cabin.

"Thank You, Lawd!" I said out loud. "This ain't exactly the Holiday Inn, but it's better'n nothin'."

Now it was starting to rain. I could hear thunder raging in the distance. The sky was so black, I could hardly see my hands before me. I was scared as a fly caught in a spider's web. In other words, I was scared as pure heck; not of being lost, or being swept away by some strong gust of wind, but of all the gory monsters Big Ma would sit by her old wood stove and tell me about while plaiting my hair..

She'd settle herself in that old flowered arm chair, with her broad hips pressing against the sides and proceed to give me the lowdown about things that only folks in the low country knew. About ghosts that lived in old, abandoned houses, and didn't like being disturbed. About witch doctors who always lived in secluded, old shacks, way back in the woods . . . who had all kinds of spells cast around the outside of their homes to ward off intruders . . . especially, uninvited ones.

When Big Ma was telling one of her spine tingling stories about *'People who practice de Devil's work'* her favorite phrase was, *"Dem ghosts of folks wit' lost souls an' dem witch doctors is some mean cusses in dis world. An' de best thang for you tuh do is to keep yo' distance from their territory. You kno' w'at I mean? Dem witch doctors kin put a root on you an' make you crawl 'roun' on de ground like a snake, an' heave up lizards an' scorpions. Dey always carry black cat bones, chicken feet, an' JuJu beads tuh keep they Mo-Jo workin' an' protect dem from ev'rythang from serious illness tuh losing money So let me say it one mo' time,* **keep yo' distance**!"

By the time she was done, I was more scared than ever and I started thinking out loud, "I can't wait to see Valerie Jackson again, 'cause when I do, I'm gon' kick her behind all the way from Cates Middle School to Pickett Farm Road an' back."

Another clap of thunder brought me back to reality. It shook the entire cabin. I ran inside and slammed the door behind me. I scanned the tiny, one-room dwelling. The ceiling was littered with cracks and crevices. *"The rain'll start to pour in soon,"* I thought to myself. In front of me was an old rock fireplace. *Must be used by hunters,* I assumed.

A small pile of wood was stacked on the floor, on the left side of the fireplace.

I noticed a cutting chill in the air inside the cabin. I imagined how nice a roaring fire in that fireplace would be.

A match, I thought to myself. *If only I could find a match.*

I dug deep into my red and white, plaid book bag. "Lawd, please let me find a book of matches in here," I prayed out loud. "There's gotta be a book of matches in here somewhere. All them times me an' Val sneaked 'round the back of the stable to smoke them Pall Mall cigarettes I'd stolen from that cupboard in the dinin' room, where Pa kept 'em. There's gotta be a match in here somewhere. Just let me find one match."

My hand brushed against a familiar surface. I snatched the book of matches from the bag and opened it.

"Two damned matches!" I swore out loud. I threw my hands over my mouth. "Lawd hammercy!" I begged. "Please forgive me for sayin' a bad word. I didn't mean to swear in Yo' presence, Lawd. An' if You just let me git out of this here mess in one piece, Lawd, I swear, I'll never cuss again long as I live. I'll raise my hand an' swear on a whole stack of the Good Book as soon as I git out of here. I'll be good as a' angel from here on."

I pulled a handful of papers from my book bag and stuffed them on top of the grate in the fireplace. Then I piled wood on top of the papers. I struck the first match against the rough surface on the side of the box. It lit in an instance. The wind promptly blew it out.

I stared at the last match in my trembling hand. I thought to myself, *this is my last chance.*

I looked up at the ceiling again. "Lawd, I swear . . ."

I took another sheet of paper from the book bag and twisted it tightly at both ends. I bent down to the fireplace and held the match closely to my body. I struck it against the side of the box and watched it light. I held the match up to the paper and watched the flame grab hold of the twisted end and flicker as I held it downward and made contact with the paper stuffed under the wood. The papers caught fire. The wood ignited. The bright light from the fire illuminated the room; the chill left the air.

The wind continued to whistle and howl against the sides of the fragile cabin. The lightning continued to flash and light up the entire forest. I was so exhausted; I spread my jacket over me and fell asleep on the floor in front of the fireplace.

I'm not sure how long I'd been asleep before a deafening roar of thunder rumbled throughout the forest and startled me so, I sprang to my feet in a single leap and noticed the fire was about to go out.

I threw the last few logs onto the red embers and sat down on the feather mattress covering the army-type cot that was pushed against the wall, under the only tiny window in the cabin. I tucked my arms under my jacket with the back around the front of my body, and fell back onto the bed. The ceiling stared down at me.

The wind was stronger than ever. The walls of the cabin cracked with each assaulting gust.

Suddenly, there was a glaring beam of lightning that flashed through the window and literally blinded me, and a crackling noise that made my ears ring and intensified with every passing second. I turned my head to the right and saw splinters skidding down the side of the wall.

All I could imagine was *the roof was cavin' in!* Pieces of tile heaped onto the floor in slow motion. Then the right side of the cabin started to cave in . . . all in very slow motion.

I was virtually glued to the bed. The only portion of my body that had not fallen victim to total paralysis were my eyes, as they stared appallingly at the rustic structure falling down around me.

All my mind could reflect was, *I'm gonna die. This is it!*

I felt the terror in my eyes intensify as the tree came into view. My first thought was, *it's huge, almost as big as the cabin.* The tree fell even slower than the shingles that were piled on the floor.

The lightning had dissected the tree from its roots, and it was, very slowly, crashing through the roof of the cabin. It was as if my entire surroundings had slowed down to a fraction of their normal pace.

I tried to move, to scream. No response. I resigned myself to the very ugly fact that the monstrous oak would come crashing down on me and flatten me like dough under a rolling pin. It fell so leisurely, it was difficult to believe that it was falling at all, as it slowly but surely, cascaded closer and closer to its defenseless victim. I closed my eyes and thought to myself, *If this woody monster's gon' squash me like a bug, I ain't gotta watch,* but reflex made me reopen them. There it was, twenty tons of pure solid oak, twenty feet from my paralyzed frame.

My life flashed before me. I saw myself, the ringleader, smoking in the hayloft with a half dozen neighborhood kids. I saw the cigarette fall from Edna's hand, onto the bale of hay. I saw the blaze rising to the roof of the stable, and the horses scurrying about, trying to escape the raging flames, and every child, except me, gittin' the spanking of their lives.

"No one, but God, an' the seven of us kids, ever knew how that fire got started."

I whispered to myself. "Lawd, I'll never smoke another cigarette long as I live." I continue. "Án' that time I chewed some of Pa's Black Maria Sweet Chewin' Tobacco . . . bit off a big wad. It tasted like crap. An' me, bein' the dumb, stupid, iggn'ant child that I was, I went an' swallowed the spit. An' when I come back to my senses, I swear! I'd done took me a trip to the moon an' back."

I closed my eyes once more and managed to turn on my right side. The next thing I knew, I was falling through space. The floor came up and slapped me, hard, in the face.

I sat up, blinked twice, and rubbed both eyes. On the floor beside me was that old, black doll, with the missing arm, that I got on my sixth birthday. I ripped that left arm off one day in one of my usual fits of anger.

My old baby crib, with half the spindles missing, stood in a corner in front of me . . . a flaming red blanket tucked tightly around the edges of the mattress. A neon sign, on the wall above it, in bright, red letters, spelled out **W-E-L-C-O-M-E!**

I felt miserably warm. The temperature seemed to swelter close to 150^0. *Uncommonly hot for this time of the year*, I thought to myself, as I continued to scan my surroundings.

To the left of the crib was a black, steel door. Steamy heat generated from it like an old boiler radiator.

Before I could blink, the door started to slowly glide open from the middle, like the doors to an elevator. ...And there He stood, in all His unsavory glory. Lucifer Himself. In the red, hot-blooded flesh! Pitchfork in hand. Maliciously grinning from ear to ear.

His twirling eyes looked like red balls of fire, bouncing clock-wise circles of light from wall to wall.

I stared in sheer delight. "Well, I'll be doggoned!" I lyriced, "if it ain't ol' Lucifer, Hisself. You ol' Son-Of-A-Gun! Did I keep you waitin'?"

He extended his right hand out to me. His seven inch long nails glittered in the light of His rotating eyes.

"Come along, my Princess," He bellowed. "We've long awaited your arrival. We have lots of 'Hell Raisin' to do."

I rose from the floor.

"I'll just bet you have, You ol' snake-bellied serpent, You!"

I paused for a moment, then stretched both arms way out to the sides.

"Well, here I am," I boasted, "In all my glory! I'm ready when you are, Brother, Luke."

He wrapped a long, black cloak around my shoulders. We strolled through the steel doors. They closed behind us.

I made a complete 360^0 circle as I perused my new surroundings. An unnerving calm filled the air. There were no ceilings to limit my view of the wild, endless dark yonder. There were no walls or boundaries as far as the eye could see.

"What a strange new world," I uttered in sheer wonderment. I felt somewhat like a free-range chicken.

Lucifer took hold of my left hand and turned the palm of his left hand upward. Then he fanned it outward as he spoke, "This is your kingdom, my Lovely. I shall entitle you my Rib. Your reign will be eternal."

"Do you mean that I can do as I please, Brother, Luke?" I asked ever so innocently.

"Yes it does, my Lovely. This is your kingdom to rule as you so desire."

"Then I so desire to liven up this here place, if you don't mind, Brother, Luke. I'm all for raisin' a lil hell an' tossin' a lil fire an' brimstones, so, no offense, my man, this place is deader than cold soup on a winter day. No insult intended."

"None taken, my Lovely. Just remember who's the Boss and who's the Rib. In other words, don't forget your place."

I walked off and mumbled, "Hell, this place is no better'n up there."

Ol' Lucifer asked, "What you say?"

"Oh, nothin'," I lied. "I just said this much better'n up there."

Lucifer smiled and nodded his head, not knowing to what degree he'd offended me. And when I'm offended, I get revenge. I went into full combat mode and decided to turn all those lifeless creatures walking 'round like Zombies, into full-fledged mutineers.

From then on, there was nothing but hot fun in the never ending summer time. Heat waves and all kinds of fire and brimstones being tossed about. All aimed at ol' Lucifer. I had declared open war on Satan.

A broad smile came over my face. I yelled out, "Look out now! Sister Ribella's in town. This here's my kinda place. Hot, sweltering, bone scorching, nonstop, mortal agony. Hot damned!"

I thought to myself, *Lucifer gave me this here power, so I may as well make the best of it, an' dance these lifeless demons right outta town an' replace them wit' some real live hellions .*

I reached down, picked up a handful of dirt, rolled it into a ball, spat on it, and turned it into a flaming sphere of molten lava. I tossed it into a crowd and watched the smoke rise fifty feet into the air.

I waved my hand and commanded, "Let there be life in Hell as t'was on Earth."

The group turned into a clan of Scottish folk dancers, wearing brightly colored, plaid kilts and knee-high socks.

I tossed balls of fire into the next group, and the next, and the next.

By the time I was done there was a lively group of people, doing as many kinds of dances in Hell as there were on Earth.

First came the three-foot-tall Elves, dressed in green, doing an Irish Polka and country women, wearing floor-length dresses and aprons, doing the Halla-Walla swing with no partners. And Greek village dancers, squatting and bouncing about, wearing bright red costumes and pointy shoes, with tassels on the toes.

There were Roman jugglers, dancing and performing acrobatics. And school children, in elaborate costumes, playing and singing, "Ring around the Rosies; Pocket Full of Posies . . ."

Then came the African American slaves, dressed in classy costumes, engaged in high-stepping strolls, called Cakewalks, poking fun at their Massa.

I can't leave out the Charleston street dancers doing the Jitterbug, and latch key kids in Spanish Harlem, tap dancing on the city sidewalks, all of whose faces look like they were molded from the face of Satan.

All of those once condemned souls having the time of their lives made Ol' Lucifer mad enough to spit fire.

"What the devil have you done to my kingdom?" he roared.

"I just thought I'd liven up the place a lil, that's all," I said, in a very fake, innocent voice. "I didn't mean no harm. I was just tryin' to help. I'm so sorry. Will you forgive me? I didn't mean no harm. Please give me another chance."

"Okay. Stop begging. I'll give you one more chance. But if you ever betray me again, I will condemn you to never ending doom up there. Do I make myself clear?"

"Yessuh, Massa, Luke."

"Now return my Kingdom back to the Hellish state that you found it. Toss around some real demon-inducing fire and brimstones. Make me proud to call you my Rib."

I thought to myself, *be very careful what you ask for. You just might git it an' won't know what the dickens to do wit' it.*

Being the lil devil that I was, I gave Him what he asked for. I tossed plenty of fire and brimstones, right at Him, with a lil help from my new, best friends.

I got the Harlem tap dancing kids making Him tap dance and do splits, trying to dodge all those balls of fire they tossed in his direction.

The Scottish folk dancers overpowered Satan and dressed him in a red, white, and blue checkered kilt with striped knee-high socks. They handed him the bagpipes and ordered him to, "Play us a high stepping tune and get rid of some of that hot air you been carrying around."

The three-foot-tall elves created a totem pole standing on each other's shoulders, jumped on Satan's back and wrestled him down to the ground on all fours. They straddled his back and pressed him to ride them around in a circle like a carnival pony. Then he reared up on his knees on command, and neighed like a horse.

Now it was the country women's turn who clearly had forgotten all about Southern hospitality. They huddled tightly around Satan like a team of linebackers. When he emerged from the crowd, they'd dressed him a baby-blue bonnet and a floor-length gown with the bottom resembling an open umbrella. They each took a spin with him on the floor before releasing him into the merciless hands of the Roman jugglers. They picked him up and tossed him so high into the air, more than a dozen times, it left his head spinning when he finally landed on the ground, head first.

While he was stretched out on the rock solid turf, trying to come back to his senses, the elaborately dressed school kids continued their childish jingle, singing;

"Dance around the rose,
Satan got stank toes
North side, South side
Old Satan fell down . . ."

The African-American slaves carried on their high-stepping Cakewalk, dancing and skipping around Satan, sticking their tongues out at him, chanting,

"Look at ol' Lucifer
Laying on the groun'
He fell down an'
Cracked His crown"
Shake it tuh de east
Shake it tuh de west

Shake it tuh de devil

Dat you loves de best…."

Then they all turned around and shook their backsides in his face.

The Charleston Jitter-buggers took Satan's embarrassment to a whole new level when they yanked him from the ground, twirling and swinging him from one person to the next, until he was finally able to stagger from amongst the group of mutinous souls.

Satan was mad as pure divine hell. His humiliation before millions of formerly condemned souls had no bounds.

I thought to myself, *"Oh, amazin' disgrace, how sweet to bring Satan to the ground."*

I knew I had to watch my back from then on. Ol' Satan would be out to get me for sure. He did just the opposite and started singing and kicking up his heels along with the other dancers in the streets. I let my guards down and joined them.

Ol Lucifer flicked His wrist and every kind of flowers imaginable, daisies, and tulips, and orchids, and all grades of blooms, rained down from the sky. We danced and twirled for hours and my red, flair-tail gown floated in the air.

I was so lost in the music and dancing I failed to notice that Ol' Lucifer was slowly leading me back to the door that I came through when I first arrived. The door opened before I realized where I was. Ol' Lucifer looked at me and said, "Nobody rules this Kingdom but Me, you little Tart. I warned you never to betray me again, or I'd condemn you to eternal damnation on Earth." Then he shoved me hard on the shoulders and said, "Enjoy the free ride, my Lovely. Ain't enough room in this hell hole for the both of us. So long, Baby!"

As the funnel cloud developed from above and began to suck me upward, I started screaming and cussing to the top of my lungs. "You no-good, stank breath, slithering snake. I'll be back. And the next time, I'm comin' wit' plenty of back-up. Just you wait an' see!"

His rumbling laughter faded into my frightful shrill as I'm lifted backwards through a seemingly endless tunnel.

Before I was out of full range of his voice, I heard Satan's bold command to the Almighty. "As long as You sit on Your throne on high, don't You ever send that she-devil down here again. This place will never be big enough for the both of us. It took a whole lot of devil to pull off a stunt like that, but she made me look like a pure, divine fool down here in the underworld. I don't care what it takes, but do what You have to. Turn her into a saint, a good Samaritan, or the Queen of Sheba. I don't care. Just make sure that the next time she meets with an untimely death, she goes to Heaven 'cause she can't ever come back down here again. Not ever! In other words, she has permanently worn out her W-E-L-C-O-M-E in this town"

Just when I thought my north bound journey would go on forever, my position shifted and I slammed face first, onto the floor. I raised my head and realized I was back in the cabin.

The storm was over. The red cinders in the fireplace had kept the cabin warm. And streaks of the new morning sun were peeking through the cracks in the cabin walls that were miraculously still standing.

There may have been gale force winds, but no giant oak had crashed through the roof of the cabin, and, **"Halle'lullah**!," I shouted, as I jumped up and danced around the room, glad as all heck that I had not dance with the Devil.

What could I say but

"SON-OF-YO'-MAMA'S-LOVER!"

"BLOW ME DOWN!!"

"GO TO HECK FIRE!"

"I'M BACK ON HOME TURF!"

Thought I'd never see another rainy night in Georgia.

"Whew! Thank You, Lawdy. I promise to be the best Servant you ever had. Amen."
Halle'lullah! It was all just a bad dream"!

TOSSIN' TOBACCO WORMS

It was just six a.m. when I headed down the hill towards the barn to start a long day of handing tobacco leaves. Will West was already standing under the shed wearing a devilish grin with his hands locked behind him. I knew right away that he was up to no good, so I asked, "Why you standing there showing all thirty two of yo' teeth, grinning like a horse eatin' briars?"

Will brought his right hand forward and opened it up, one finger at a time, and the worm came into view.

"You throw that doggone tobacco worm on me, I'm gon' beat the tar outta you, so help me, Moses!" I threatened.

"You ain't scared of no lil, green worm, is you, girly? I didn't think you was scared of nothin', not even the devil hisself. Look at all these lil white eggs all over her back. That means she gon' have a hundred lil baby worms crawling 'round in just a few days."

The next thing Will did was downright gross, even for someone as disgusting as he. He brought the worm up to his mouth, bit off the head, and spat it out on the ground. He looked up at me and the smile got bigger. All he said was, "Here, catch."

Before I could step back out of the path of that flying insect, it slammed into the front of my shirt. Worm blood spread across my top like green ink and it stuck there like glue. I had to scrape it off with the tobacco stick I'd picked up to frail the devil out of Will's head with.

When Will saw me coming toward him, he turned and ran. Fear caused him to look back and see how close I was, and he ended up getting tangled in the spool of tobacco thread, looped over the support beam beside the tobacco slide.

"Good for you," I yelled out, just before I started frailing his back with both hands, all the while listening to him crying and begging like a little girl.

Every time the stick landed on his back, I called him a different name, "You igg'nant, thick-headed dummy! When God was giving out sense, you musta been sleepin' in the next room. Ain't you figured out yet that when I say 'no' I mean 'no', an' if you don't listen to me, you gon' git the crap beat out of you? Then you gon' go running home to yo' mammy, sobbing like a baby, when it's all over."

I kept on frailing, at the same time asking, "You had 'nough, dummy? Or do you want some mo'?"

Then I started kicking him from front to back, while he rolled from side to side, trying to duck each strike of my solid toed shoe. Every time he rolled over, he tangled himself more and more in that spool of thread.

I gave him one last kick and he ended up rolling all the way to the bottom of the hill and landed in the ditch. I got tired of hearing him gasp for breath, so I took the little saw, hanging on the side of the barn, and cut the thread. When he unraveled that thread from around his neck, he scrambled to his feet and headed for home, talking trash that he didn't think I could hear. "You don't know me, gal. I'm from Bearpond!"

I asked, "What you say?"

He took off running like hogs racing to the slop trough.

I walked back up the hill to the barn, mumbling to myself in response to his pathetic revelation. "And you don't know me either" I said "I'm from Gillsiden and I'll slice you like a side of salty pork and feed you to these boney hound dawgs!"

Then I started putting sticks on the two racks on both sides of the slide and waited for the ladies to come and start wrapping the tobacco, just like nothing ever happened.

My mama, Miss Helen Clark, Mabel Massenburg, and Mrs. Vidalia Dawson are about the fastest tobacco wrappers I've ever seen. They each have three people handing tobacco to them, including me, and they work the pure daylights out of us. They can clear a full slide of tobacco in less than ten minutes. My poor arms would be turning like a Ferris wheel, grabbing a bundle of tobacco from the slide passing it on to them, rocking from side to side, flipping that tobacco over that stick like they we're tossing pancakes.

The only rest we got from the time we started, before sunlight, until we broke for lunch, was when they changed the empty slide for another full one. And the slides just kept coming and coming.

All of the primers and wrappers ate lunch at our house, so Ma always stopped at eleven to go to the house and finish fixing the food she started around 4:00 a.m. I was so glad to see the primers coming to the barn with the mules pulling that last slide for the morning; I didn't know what to do.

I started handing tobacco leaves even faster because I knew as soon as we were done with that last slide, we could go eat and get a short rest.

The day when I acquired the worm phobia, I was showing off my climbing skills, making my way to the top of a fifty foot, live oak on the front right side of the house. My cousin, Muskrat was sitting at the top waiting for me, challenging me to make it all the way up.

"I don't think you can do it. Girls can't climb no tree. The minute they git their dress caught on a limb, they start crying like a big baby 'cause they put a hole in their pretty, lil frock."

Then he started singing, "You can't do it. You can't do it."

I said, "Just you watch me. I'm gon' climb this tree all the way to the top, and slap yo' thick head all the way back to the ground."

I grabbed hold of one limb after another, hoisting myself closer and closer to Muskrat, sitting at the top of the tree, egging me on.

When I slid up on the limb beside him, he wrapped his left arm around my back, touched my shoulder, then quickly jerked it away and started climbing back down the tree. I could still feel the sensation of something on my shoulder, even though both of Muskrat's hands were busy climbing down the tree. I turned my head to see what it was. It was the biggest, fat, ugly, green Cinnamon Bull, (tobacco worm), that I ever did see, sitting on my shoulder staring at me with two horns on his head.

(I have no earthly idea why we called that worm a Cinnamon Bull, unless it was because of the red horn on either side of its head).

Muskrat yelled up at me and said, "If that thar Cinnamon Bull bites you, you gon' turn into a blood-sucking vampire and start running 'round biting folks on the neck like a mad dawg."

After Muskrat made his frightening prediction about the worm's bite turning me into some blood-thirsty beast, reflex caused me to scrape my right hand across my shoulder and swat down on the horned vermin with brute force. When I lifted my hand, there was nothing but green, squishy guts all over my shoulder, and a generous specimen of my own flesh embedded under my nails, which left my skin stinging from the scratches.

Before I took the time to contemplate the painful consequences, I bailed out of the tree, landed on a huge root, and twisted my ankle so badly, I literally saw so many stars, I thought it was the Fourth of July. The pain was so intense, it sent shock waves throughout my entire body. I screamed to the top of my lungs, yelling, "Ma! Ma!" and calling Muskrat every cuss word in the book. I swore to him, "I raise my hand 'fo God, I'm gon' pay you back for this, if it's the last thing I do. Take my word!"

Ma came running out of the front door, wiping her hands on her apron. I laid on the ground, clutching my ankle. "What happened to you, baby?" she asked. "Did you fall an' hurt yo' ankle?" I couldn't even offer a response. I just nodded my head.

T-Bone and Lemon carried me into the house and sat me on the settee, and poor Ma got another chance to practice her doctoring skills; which happened way too often for comfort. Ma tore up an old sheet, folded it over twice into a home-made bandage, soaked it in liniment, and wrapped it tightly around my ankle. She instructed me to, "Keep it up on this pillow to keep down the swelling." Then she brought me a glass of cold milk and some freshly baked tea cakes, which miraculously caused the excruciating, throbbing pain to disappear. Of course hearing Uncle Mace whip the snot out of Muskrat with a Mulberry switch, after I told him how Muskrat made me twist my ankle, had its own healing effect.

Muskrat thought he had found himself a good hiding place from the wrath of Uncle Mace behind the closet curtain, but the big dummy's shoes were sticking from under the curtains in plain sight of everybody. Uncle Mace yelled out, "Muskrat, come from behind that curtain and go out there and git me a long switch from that Mulberry tree. And if t'ain't long 'nough, I'm gon' make you git two, and keep on gittin' 'em 'til I think it's long 'nough. So you better make sure it's long 'nough the first time, if you know what's good for you."

Muskrat dropped his head and moved towards the door. His body language looked like a man headed for the gallows.

When Muskrat returned with a very long switch, Uncle Mace ordered him to, "Go back outside and shave all them leaves off that switch and meet me in the wood shed."

Poor Muskrat dropped his head again and headed back out the front door. Uncle Mace went out the back. A few minutes later I heard Uncle Mace say, "Drop them there pants! And the next time you gits the notion to scare somebody outta the top of a fifty foot tree, you better think about it twice."

The next sounds I heard were that switch whistling in the air, and Muskrat yelling out every be-good promise in the book. "I promise not to do it ag'in, Daddy," he lied. Uncle Mace knew better, and the switch kept on whistling in the air until Uncle Mace's arm got tired. The minute the switch stopped whistling, the promises stopped being made.

Muskrat came back into the house holding both sides of his butt, giving me the evil eye. I stuck my tongue out at him, and teased him saying, "Gon' be a long time 'fo' you can sit on that butt ag'in, thick-headed dummy!"

Muskrat looked at me and said, "I bet your ankle hurt more'n my butt do."

I argued back asking, "How'd you like for my good foot to kick yo' butt? And I hope you don't think this is the end of it cause I ain't got even wit' you yet. And you know that whippin' you just got from Uncle Mace won't nothin'. Wait 'til I git you, and I will git you back, you can count on it." I stuck my tongue out at him again and repeated, "Big dummy."

Uncle Mace came back inside, looked at me and said, "I bet he won't ever do that ag'in." He looked at Muskrat and ordered him to, "Git yo' things so I can take yo' behind home. You know you got another whipping coming when I tell yo' Ma what you done."

The next time I laid eyes on a big, fat ugly, green tobacco worm, I was handing leaves at that same barn where I whipped the dickens out of Will West.

I was rocking from side to side with a little rhythm in my hips, as I grabbed one bundle after another of big, green tobacco leaves, passing them on to Mrs. Vidalia Dawson. She would wrap the thread around the stems and flip the bundle over the stick, like she was braiding hair.

I stretched my hand out for another bundle when I saw one of the leaves move. Then I spotted a green head coming to the surface.

We stared each other straight in the eyes. He stared me down. I retreated to the front yard and told Skimpy Jones, "I ain't going back to that barn 'til somebody send that critter to worm hell." Skimpy agreed to do the honors and jokingly said, "Come on, I'll put him outta yo' misery."

I followed him back to the barn and watched him squash that tobacco worm under those clod-hopping boots they all wear to the field. Then he tossed the worm into the grass, where it promptly blended in with the green landscape and disappeared.

From that day on, whenever I had the job of handing tobacco leaves, I grew an extra pair of eyes, and could spot a tobacco worm at one hundred paces. And if there was a tobacco worm sighting, somebody was enlisted to turn the squirmy pest into squished up green slime.

I've seen tobacco worms grow up to three inches long and as plump as a grown man's thumb. The longer they are, the more the sight of one makes me quiver. And, needless to say, once the word got around that I was terrified of them, every guy on the farm wanted to terrorize me with every tobacco worm they could find. And being boys, some of them had to learn the hard way, that I meant it when I said, "If you put that #!*#!* tobacco worm on me, this here stick's going up side yo' head."

I remember one late summer day when Joe Watkins chased me from one barn to another, with a tobacco worm so fat, I could have sworn it was on steroids. He was trying to put it down my back, and I was running for dear life. When I looked back to see how far he was behind me, and realized he was too close for me to out run him, I stopped, turned around and gave him a head butt so hard, it made his nose bleed. When he fell straight back on the ground, I straddled him and got a choke hold on his throat. The only reason I stopped squeezing was to wipe his drool off my hands.

When I let go of his neck, he jumped up and headed for home, cussing me like a sailor and running like somebody being chased by a swarm of killer bees. I was so mad, I followed him home, went up in his house and beat the heck out of him with the broom. The whole time he was crying like a girl, yelling, "Ouch! Ouch! I ain't gon' do it no mo'." I didn't believe a word of it, so I kept on swinging until the broom broke into three pieces. A sharp point on the broom handle cut a one-inch gash on his neck. I looked him in the eyes and said, "You tell a living soul, and I'll come back and finish the job. You git my meaning?" Between the whimpers, he managed to mumble, "Uh huh." I turned and walked out the back door. He still wears that scar to this day. It's a constant reminder not to mess with this squeamish, country child. He could have spared himself a serious beat down, if he'd only consulted with a few friends first, like; Dan Johnson, whose face was rammed into the side of a tobacco slide; Rafe Robertson, who wears a one-inch scar over his right eye, after he ran head-on into a barbed wire post; Alfonso Hunter, who will never have good sense again, because a baseball bat knocked out two thirds of what little he had.

They can all tell him about the consequences of chasing me with tobacco worms, because each of them wear a skin souvenir due to the wrath of Pru.

A few weeks went by before I came up with the brilliant scheme to pay Muskrat back for prêt near making me break my neck, jumping out of that tree. I had Will West to thank for the sudden brainstorm, after I recalled how disgusting it was watching him bite off that worm's head and spit it out. I just decided to take it a step further.

I couldn't pull off the job on my own because it would involve handling a bunch of tobacco worms. I knew I could enlist the help of my good buddy Skimpy, who was all too happy to assist, by gathering a small mason jar of plump, leafy-green tobacco worms.

I gave him a piece of Ma's cheese cloth, an old, rusted potato masher, and a tin pan to press every drop of green juice he could from the creepy crawlers. I didn't have the stomach to watch, so he went around the side of the house to do the job. After straining the liquid through the cheese cloth, he poured the juice from the pan back into the jar, sat the pan with the residue beside the house, and quickly reappeared in the kitchen.

I knew that Muskrat loved lime Cool-Aid, so I was sure I'd have no problem getting him to swallow every drop of the sugar-sweet refreshment I'd concocted for him.

When I saw Muskrat coming up the path, I took the small pitcher from the cupboard and filled it with water. I emptied the pack of the lime Cool-Aid into the pitcher and Skimpy added the worm juice. I scooped up a generous amount of sugar, poured it into the mix, and gave it a good stirring with the small stick I'd picked up in the back yard. Then I dropped the stick in the wood box next to the stove and quickly refilled the same jar that held the worm juice, with the Cool-Aid.

When Muskrat stepped into the kitchen, I extended my hand with the jar of Cool-Aid and said, "Cousin, I ain't gon' keep carrying 'round this heavy grudge. I made you yo' favorite drink as a peace offerin'. Let's just bury the hatchet an' forgit the whole thing wit' the worm ever happened, okay?"

The big dummy took the bait without hesitation and swallowed the pint-sized jar of liquid in one big, long gulp.

He let out a loud, disgusting burp, wiped his mouth on his sleeve and said, "Thanks, cousin. That tastes like another one," and I promptly obliged and poured every last drop of Cool-Aid left in the pitcher into the jar..

After he slurped up the second glass I asked, "Muskrat, would you ever eat a worm?"

He made an ugly face and replied, "Ugh! Not on yo' young, spooky life. That's too nasty to even think 'bout. What made you ask that?" He inquired.

"Oh, I was just curious 'bout how you'd feel if somebody made you eat worms. I guess you wouldn't like it too much, would you?"

His response was swift with a bit of suspicion in his voice. "Naw. I'd git sick as a dawg and throw 'em right back up."

"No kidding?" I asked. "I didn't think nothing could make you sick. Yo' stomach made of lead. I never saw you throw up anything in yo' whole life. And I don't expect you to throw up that lime Cool-Aid you just swallowed wit' all that mashed up tobacco worm juice in it either. T'was real tasty won't it?"

"You lyin'!" he snapped.

"Oh, yea. You think so, huh? Well, would you like to see the green proof?" I asked. Then I looked at Skimpy and said "Why don't you show him the leftovers, Skimpy?"

He darted around the corner of the house and returned in a flash with the worm residue in the bottom of the tin pan. I still couldn't look when Skimpy extended the pan with the green mush out to Muskrat and said, "See?" while I looked the other way. Muskrat grabbed his throat and ran out the back door, gagging his head off. Not a drop of that Cool-Aid came back. I couldn't resist the urge to taunt him a little more and said, "I told you t'won't coming back up. I guess it's just gon' have to stay down there 'til it turns into pee and you piss it out." I paused for a second, then continued, "Like I said, I'll git you back if it's the last thing I do. So guess what? 'Got ya!' Bet you'll take yo' Daddy's advice the next time you gits the notion to put a tobacco worm on me, and think 'bout it twice. Now, go home. You big, dummy."

That's just what he did with his head hung down to his chest.

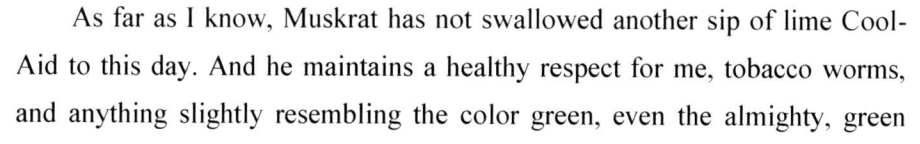

As far as I know, Muskrat has not swallowed another sip of lime Cool-Aid to this day. And he maintains a healthy respect for me, tobacco worms, and anything slightly resembling the color green, even the almighty, green dollar bill.

RINGING A TEN
(Playing Horse Shoes)

There are certain incidents, strictly accidental of course, where objects, for example, horse shoes, are tossed in the air, and unintentionally come in contact with a head, a foot, or other parts of the body, and may cause some minor bodily harm. Or in some cases, very unpleasant circumstances.

Throwing horse shoes is not an exact science you know. Say for instance, someone who swipes my last Baby Ruth candy bar from the pocket of my car-coat, might just by chance, be standing in the path of a horse shoe that, by accident, flies from the hand and slams into the back of said person's knee, knocks him to the ground, and renders him temporarily immobile. By coincidence, and of course, by accident, that's just what happened to Hewey Bolton.

Some mornings, before the sun rose, I'd help Mrs. Hazel Hawthorne pick vegetables from her garden, and sometimes, we'd pick blackberries that were still damp from the dew which brought out their sweet smelling aroma. After working for half the morning, Mrs. Hazel would give me a shiny new quarter. Made me feel countrified rich, and I'd make plans for what to spend it on. I loved Baby Ruth candy bars, so that was always the first thing on the list. I'd trek up to Whitman's General Store, buy me a rich, chewy Baby Ruth and hide it in the pocket of my carcoat so that no one else would know I had it and ask for some.

Hewey Bolton, like a lot of other neighborhood kids, loved to hang around our house and eat Ma's good cooking. He had a terrible sweet tooth, and would beg for candy or any other sugary snack if he knew you had any.

He saw me put the Baby Ruth in my coat pocket and waited until I was out of the house, took the candy bar from my pocket, and sneaked around the side of the house to eat it. Something told me to check my coat pocket because he'd been lingering inside too long. When I reached into my coat pocket, I discovered the candy bar was gone. I checked outside to see where he was and found him behind the tool shed. He saw me turn the corner and stuffed the candy into his mouth. I asked, "What you eatin', Hewey?" His mouth was so full he could barely mumble, "Nothin'."

I responded, "You lyin', Hewey. You eatin' my Baby Ruth."

He managed to swallow and lied again, "Naw, I ain't. That was my Baby Ruth. I had just bought it at the mercantile."

"You a lyin' dawg," I yelled "You know you ain't never got no money. An', besides, when you have time to go to the store? You been stickin' 'roun' here all day long. So when you have time to go to the store, Hewey?"

"Well I musta already had it in my pocket. I just forgot t'was there."

"You know somethin', Hewey, If you gon' be a liar, you aughta try an' be a goodun. I know you lyin'. You know you lyin', so why don't you just give it up. And since you done gon' an' swallowed my whole Baby Ruth, you needs to cough up a dime, and I means right now, cause you don't wanna know what I'm gon do if you don't."

Then he went insane and said, "You can't scare me. And I ain't worried 'bout you doin' nothin' to me."

I looked down and saw the four horse shoes lying on the ground. I picked up the biggest one and twirled it around on my right wrist. "If you don't want this here horse shoe to go up side yo' big, empty head, you better come up wit'a Baby Ruth candy bar, even if you gotta shoot one out yo' raw behind."

He slapped the horse shoe out of my hand and started running towards the path. I was mad enough to draw blood and started twirling the horse shoe around again and hurled it through the air, by accident of course. It sailed across the yard like a boomerang, slammed into the back of his right leg, like 'ringing a ten' on a horse shoe stake. His knees buckled. He went down to the ground, face first. I ran over to where he laid, straddled his back with my body, grabbed hold of the back of his head, and started rubbing his face on the ground. Unaware that he'd landed with his face in a fresh pile of human crap, I kept putting more and more pressure on his head each time I rubbed his face from side to side.

Then the wind shifted and I got the scent plain and clear. I grabbed a handful of Hewey's wooly-thick hair and lifted his face off of the ground. Dark-brown doo-doo was pasted all over it, with partially-chewed-up pieces of peanuts imbedded in the mix.

I quickly realized that someone else had stolen my Baby Ruth and was in such a hurry to dispose of it, they only half-chewed the candy bar and left most of the peanut fragments untouched. It couldn't have been Hewey because the candy bar he'd just eaten hadn't even had enough time to digest. It serves him right that he was wrongly accused of committing yet another act of thievery. He'd earned himself a reputation for having sticky fingers; so naturally, he'd be the first suspect when something came up missing.

I untangled my hand from Hewey's hair, released my grip, and let his head fall back to the ground, into the pile of reeking human waste.

Being the young she devil that I was, and not even about to compromise my flawless integrity, rather than say to Hewey, "I'm sorry. I made a mistake. Someone else musta stolen my Baby Ruth, ate it, and dumped it in this pile of crap, along with everything else they ate," I said instead, "You wanted yo'self a nice, gooey, chocolaty Baby Ruth candy bar, well, you got a' extra one on the side, wit' peanuts and all. Hope you enjoyed 'em both."

Hewey got up, ran a few feet, and stopped, puking like a dog. He started running again, but only got a few more feet before he had to stop and puke again. He ran, stopped, and puked until he disappeared behind the stable near the pack house.

The next morning I heard that Hewey was in the hospital. Of course my inquisitive nature caused me to investigate and find out why.

I saw Skeeter Jones, Hewey's cousin, coming down the path past the pack house and asked him what happened to Hewey? Skeeter gave me the whole story.

"Somethin' made Hewey real sick yestiddy," Skeeter said. "He come home sick and puking like a dawg. He got up this mornin' still sick and puking like a dawg. Nothin' Aunt Carrie gave him helped. So they put him in the truck and hauled him off to the doctor. Doctor tells them he done puked so much he got dehydrated. They had to put him in the hospital and give him fluids to git him back right. I heard it from my brother, Jock, that they on their way back home right now."

"I wonder what happened to him?" I asked ever so innocently.

"Don't know. And he won't say."

"He knows better," I mumbled.

"What's that?" Skeeter asked.

"Oh, nothin'," I lied. "I just said 'hope he's better'."

When I returned home, later that day, I told Ma about Hewey's bout with the vomiting and dehydration. Her first response was, "Well, what in the world happened, sugar?"

"I ain't rightly sure, Ma," I lied, for the umpteenth time. "When I left this mornin', to go help Mrs. Hazel pick her garden stuff, she told me 'bout him bein' in the hospital. She didn't know nothin' else but that."

"Later on," I continued, "When I see'd Skeeter comin' down the path, I asked him what happened to Hewey. He said somethin' 'bout him bein' real sick the day b'fo' an' pukin' so much he lost all his body fluids an' stuff, and had to go to the hospital for them to give him some mo' fluids."

"Well I wonder what in the world you s'pose done that," she asked

I didn't have an answer for that, but I knew I had to come up with somethin' good to throw her off track.

Ma's questions were starting to git a lil too pryin'. An' I was starting to git a lil too worried that she might stumble up on the truth. And I ain't gotta tell you what kinda paddlin' my backsides would git if that happened.

So I slightly changed the subject, and said, "You think he gon' be alright, Ma?"

"I don't know, baby. Losin' yo' body fluids like that can set you back a ways. He gon' be feelin' mighty weak for a while."

Then the false angel in me came out, and I said, "You think we oughta pray for him, Ma?"

"T'won't hurt none, baby. Prayer always be a good thang. Yea," Ma repeated, "I think prayin' for him will be a real good thang. That's very kind of you to ask. I'm sure he'll 'ppreciate it. Why don't you start it off."

"Yes, Ma'am. In the name of our Savior, we ask you to look over our friend, Hewey, an' make sure he comes through this sickness and makes a full recovery. We asks you to forgive our sins and make us numb so we don't feel the pain of livin' in this unsanctified world. In the name of our Savior, Amen."

"That was lovely, Princess," Ma praised me. She didn't know that prayer was more for me than Hewey. My butt was in for a serious whipping, if she found out that I was the one who caused Hewey to do all that pukin' that lead to him bein' dehydrated and ending up in the hospital. I just hoped she didn't hold her breath waiting for a confession from me.

Fortunately, Hewey came through with flying colors. Unfortunately for me, Hewey gave Ma all the details of his non-accidental condition.

I knew I was in trouble when I heard her bellow from the kitchen. I was overcome with the temptation to do what my sister, Genevieve, did when Ma called her full name, and she'd run for Hell and high water, straight to the corn field. But, being the stubborn, partially insane child that I was, when I heard, "Pandora Lucinda Marshall, come here!" instead of running in the opposite direction, I strutted straight toward the more than threatening voice. I only made it to the front porch before she met me at the door, took me by the hand, and lead me back down the steps to the honey suckle bush on the side of the dining room. With just one yank, she snatched off the longest limb on the entire bush, and with another sweep, every leaf on the switch ended up on the ground.

She pulled my dress tight around my butt and started swinging, all the while ordering me, saying, "Tell me you ain't gon' do it ag'in!" She made that command a half dozen times. I never said a word, but stood there looking like some inflated pond frog, sitting on a lily pad ready to start croaking. It hurt like the pure dickens, but I was not about to let her know it. After about ten frails, she just gave up, looked at me, shook her head, glanced up at the sky, and prayed, "Lawd, I leave her in Yo' hands, cause she needs mo' help than I can give her!" Then she dropped the switch on the ground and walked back into the house.

Hewey never stole another one of my Baby Ruth candy bars. In fact, I don't think he's stolen another thing to this day.

He grew up. Went to the Southern Baptist Seminary and became an Ordained Minister.

Now, he counsels young inmates at the Federal prison in Brookston, Tennessee, toting his personal copy of the New King James Version of the Holy Scriptures.

He preaches about the Sermon on the Mount, recites the Twenty Third Psalm, and has placed a permanent book mark in his preferred books of the Bible. Bet you can't guess which ones are his all-time favorites.

You guessed it. Deuteronomy 5:19, "Neither must you steal," and Exodus 20:15, "You must not steal." Now I'd say those were good words to live by.

I guess that accidental encounter between Hewey's face and that peanutty pile of human crap was all it took to cure him of his life-long-sugar-induced-severely-annoying case of Kleptomania.

Can I get an 'AMEN!?'

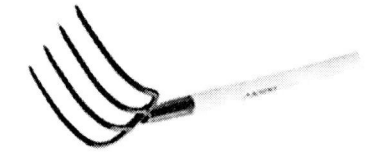

PITCHFORKS & BARE FEET

One of the most multi-functional, sometimes natural, sometimes man-made resources on any farm, is a pond. I had the distinct privilege of utilizing no less than three within near spitting distance of our house.

There was the standard sized pond right across the road in front of the house. There was the bigger one in back of the house that could have easily qualified as a small lake. And beyond that one, tucked neatly and obscurely inside a thicket of jungle standard overgrowth, was a tiny pond with the most pristine, aqua-blue water I ever saw.

Only a select few of Holt Grissom's closest friends were privy to the stocked-to-the-rim-with-brim gem, concealed just a few hundred yards in back of that large irrigation pond.

This was where he'd stashed his prized stock of the biggest brim and catfish that one could catch with any hook, line, or sinker.

I stumbled onto it one hot, summer day, while embarking upon one of my unauthorized woodland adventures. I'd approached that thick undergrowth before, which I later found out was the back entry to the pond, but due to fear of the unknown, never until then, had I conjured up the nerve to investigate the secrets that lie beyond it.

The growth was so defined, it would have been virtually impossible for a full grown adult to penetrate it. It had an entry way that was less than two feet in diameter. I had to literally get down on my hands and knees and crawl and slide on my belly at least a hundred feet through some of the thickest brush and briars I'd ever encountered.

By the time I reached the clearing at the end of that long, green tunnel, I was nearly covered in mud. And there was not a spot on either of my arms, my legs, and face, that didn't contain a scratch from colliding with all of that rough undergrowth. But it was well worth the agony because I had made a million dollar discovery.

What most of those self proclaimed anglers in the area wouldn't have given for the chance to throw a line into that gold mine of country seafood delight.

Needless to say, my lips were sealed shut, tight as a vice grip. I never told another living soul about my superbly hidden discovery. I, alone wanted exclusive angling rights to that first rate fishing hole. And did I ever abuse that privilege.

I completely abandoned the big pond all together. For years it had been one of my favorite places to escape the rigors of farming and household chores.

Sometimes, I would sneak across the pond dam and climb into that little dingy of a boat, that was permanently chained to a huge oak tree at the edge of the pond, and paddle it out a few feet into the water. I would sit there and catch me one good sized fish and drag it all the way back to the house.

Ma would have had a major fit if she'd known how many times I'd performed that adolescent act of defiance. I had lost track of the number of times I'd heard her say, "Boy, don't you let me catch you goin' to that pond by yo'self." And since the sturdiness of that boat was more than a little bit questionable, I shutter to think of the level of trouble I would have ended up in, for daring to row it, even one foot out into the water. In any event, her words didn't amount to a spit in the pond. I was so spoiled and bull-headed, the advice she uttered simply floated into one ear and swam out the other.

By the time I reached the house, the fish was covered with dirt, and half of its scales had already been scraped off from scuffing against all of those abrasive rocks along the path.

Although I loved sneaking down to the pond for my private fishing expedition, I'd acquired a sort of phobia about touching the fish when it was still alive, flapping about on the hook. I had once, carelessly, tried to remove a large brim from the hook, when it made a sudden twitch and out came the fins. The pain was instantaneous when one of those razor sharp floatation extensions punctured my palm so badly, it sent shock waves all the way up to my elbow.

After that eye opening experience, I never tried to take another live fish off of the hook. I'd arrive at the house with the half mutilated fish trailing behind on the line that was sometimes, a simple string of tobacco thread, and talk one of the guys, that was always hanging around our house, into cleaning it for me.

When he was done, I'd fry up the single fish, which was at times, no bigger than a playing card, once the head and tail were removed. But my appetite had been appeased, having satisfied my longing for fresh fish.

Most of the time I surmised that it was hardly worth the trouble, because there really was barely enough fish to cook. But I cooked and ate what little remained anyway.

I guess that was my way of proving to myself that I could provide for myself if the going got really rough.

I grew up somewhat like the black Tom Sawyer of the south. Being a country child, I traversed the three or more hundred acre spread bare foot from May through October. I could and would make a fishing pole out of anything that wasn't tied down. I would go to Thal Whitman's General store with less than ten cents, buy a hook and sinker for my tobacco thread fishing line, tie it to one end of a tobacco stick, and catch all the fish I could eat.

My bait was a can of the biggest, fattest earthworms I could find. And there was no better place to find a whole hefty mess of the hardy critter, than under a big pile of runny cow manure.

First, I had to shoo away the one thousand flies that had settled on top of the heap of dark, brown bovine feces. Then I'd use the pitchfork to rake away most of the pile and start digging. In less than one minute flat, the can was half full of plump, squirming earthworms. Then I'd head off to the pond, catch the maximum one fish, drag it back to the house, and find another dope to clean it for me, before cooking and eating it as usual.

Nobody ever told me how dumb it was to dig up fishing worms with a pitchfork. But, then, I probably wouldn't have listened to them if they had.

I knew it was ideal for pitching hay, hence the name 'pitchfork,' but it was my tool of choice for digging worms as well. So I hung onto the habit. That is, until the day I made a slight miscalculation in the distance between the pitchfork and me, and ended up forking my foot instead of the ground. The odd thing is, I didn't realize what I had done until after I'd been to the pond, caught my one limit fish, and was walking up the path, back to the house, dragging the fish behind me.

I remembered feeling a slight sting when I made that last stab into the soil, but I didn't pay much attention to it. What I'd done was harpoon the top of my right foot with the outermost left prong of the pitchfork.

As time went by, the stinging sensation became more and more noticeable, and halfway to the house, I looked down and stared into a gaping hole on top of my aching foot.

I imagined turning as white as the flesh exposed inside of the hole, which was the exact same dimensions as the prongs on the pitchfork.

Panic instantly set in. My heart pounded so loudly I could hear it through my own ears. Mother Nature had been rendered soundless because the throbbing pulsating banging against the walls of my chest had drowned out every bird that chirped, every frog that croaked, and every last yard chicken that clucked.

My hands shook so violently, they eventually went numb and I dropped the tobacco stick, with the thread and fish attached to it, somewhere along the path in rear of me. I don't recall if I ever went back to recover that stick and fish or not, because truth be told, I can barely remember arriving at the house.

What I do remember is the frightful look on Ma's face when I stumbled through the back door. The first words out of her mouth were, "What's the matter? What you done gone and done now?"

All of a sudden, I had been traumatized into a state of total muteness. I opened my mouth but not a single sound came out. Ma repeated the question again, but I was still unable to utter a word.

After a half dozen attempts to speak, I gave up trying to talk, and was finally able to point down at my foot.

When Ma saw the hole and all of that white meat staring up at her, she nearly fainted. But, being the always-managing-to-hold-it-together type of person that she was, she kept her cool and started another one of her home remedy routines, Johnny on the spot.

She knew instantly what had caused the unmistakable puncture to my flesh, so she didn't bother to ask how it had happened, or what had created it.

She cleaned the wound with warm water and apple cider vinegar. Then she sprinkled gun powder that she had emptied from one of Pa's 12-gauge shot gun shells, into the hole. I remember a slight stinging sensation when the gunpowder came into contact with the open wound.

After the hole was thoroughly cleaned and packed, she bandaged it with sterilize strips from an old sheet.

Every day for the next week, she'd remove the old bandage, clean out the wound with more vinegar and warm water, sprinkle fresh gunpowder into the quickly closing hole, and apply a fresh, new bandage.

During that week's time, the hole had continued to gradually close up, and on the eight day, when she removed the bandage, the hole no longer existed. All that remained was a thin scab and a tiny, little dip in the skin on top of my foot.

Ma never scolded or reprimanded me for pulling that dangerously, stupid stunt. I think she figured I'd learned a pretty good lesson from my incessant act of dull wittedness and that no affirmation from her was necessary.

My mother was, in my own biased opinion, without a doubt, the most considerate person that ever lived. And rather than cause me any embarrassment in front of the other kids, she kept the details of my foot's accidental run in with that perilous farm implement, our little secret. She knew those rambunctious ruffians would laugh me right out of town if they got wind of my absurd encounter with that pitchfork. She had a real talent for saving face. And I presented many occasions for her to save mine.

I could not, in all honesty, say that I never turned over another thick, runny pile of cow manure, or that I never dug up another batch of fat, slithering earthworms, for fishing bait. But, I will swear on a twenty-two-and-a-half-foot-long fishing pole, that I never again, used a pitchfork to do it.

Many years have gone by since that fateful day with the pitchfork, but I shall never forget that incident when our hay pitching fork forked up more than a few fat worms to bait a fish hook.

I have a daily reminder of that empty headed act of senselessness, which did, in a sense, have a silver lining, because I learned two very valuable lessons from my mindless behavior

Lesson number one: "If you need to dig up a few worms to do a little angling in the local fishing hole, please leave the pitchfork to pitching hay, and use a shovel or hoe instead. Especially if your geometric knowledge is a bit unreliable."

Lesson number two: "I learned through bitter experience that pitchforks, dark meat, and bare feet simply don't mix. They are not a good recipe for safe, aquatic recreation."

"I close my case."

BLACK MARIA

It was the year 1969 when I decided to try my hands at being an adult and sample some of the pleasures that they, exclusively, seemed privileged to enjoy.

The hay loft, on the second level of our two-story horse stable, was my favorite place on the entire farm to engage in juvenile horseplay and misfortune, because it provided the privacy and concealment necessary for petty, criminal behavior.

My first and only experiment with cigarettes was promptly renounced when one of my enlisted partners in crime, one Edna Mae Brown, smoked her unfiltered Pall Mall down to her finger, and dropped it onto a bale of hay, when the heat from the almost expended stub came into contact with his flesh. Faster than you could say, Jack rabbit, the bone dry hay went up in flames like a stack of papers, doused with kerosene. And before I and the remainder of my party of juvenile bandits could descend the 15-step ladder from the loft to the ground level of the stable, the fire had already burned a hole in the back of the stable big enough to drive one of Harv Jackson's oversized John Deere tractors through it.

Inside the house, my favorite place to rummage through was that long junk drawer, which extended across the entire front of the olive green china cabinet in our dining room. That was Pa's favorite place to stash the things that were 'off limits' to us kids. And all but I respected that consideration.

I was a rambler. And places considered 'out of my jurisdiction,' were all the more intriguing. I was more than a little bit inquisitive and often wondered if those Pall Mall cigarettes, that Black Maria Sweet Chewing Tobacco, and the Tupelo Snuff, were really as pleasurable as grownups made them out to be. So I decided to find out for myself.

Having dismissed the cigarette theory as merely a lot of 'hoopla,' and dangerous to boot, I decided to privately sample a mouthy chew of Miss. Black Maria. And eyeing the word 'sweet' on the red, gold, and black label, I imagined the taste was somewhat like that of a sweet, chewy, chocolate candy bar. That was a monumental mistake. I broke off a hefty sample of the three inch slab of processed tobacco, quickly popped it into my mouth, and began to chew.

The unanticipated bitter shock to my palate prompted a muscle reflex that sent the mouthful of repulsively slimy gook sliding down my throat, which initiated gags and convulsions. And every attempt to regurgitate the sickening concoction I had swallowed failed profoundly.

Suddenly, everything around me became mobilized. I slid down the ladder from the loft, butt first, and scrambled to my feet. I surveyed the distance from the stable to the door of the back porch. The one hundred and fifty or so feet now seemed more like a thousand.

The narrow foot path to the house had suddenly become a jungle, filled with man eating plants that had germinated to ten times their normal size. The wild onions on both sides of the path, waved like the grass blades on a Hula skirt. The puffy clouds overhead did somersaults and cartwheels, and contoured themselves into dizzying shapes and forms.

By the time I reached the door of the closed in back porch, I was literally crawling on hands and knees. I weaved my way through the maze of furniture throughout the house and ended up on the elongated, front, cement porch. I spotted the old quilt that I sometimes slept on when the summer nights became too hot to rest comfortably inside. And the last thing I remember was collapsing, face down, on a pile of cushy softness.

Then the lights went out and the fireworks began. My total anatomy became weightless and I began to rise above the pile of quilts underneath me, barely clearing the overhang of the porch as I rose above it. Within minutes, I could see the Earth's full perimeter. I must have orbited our atmosphere a half dozen times. It felt like I was being propelled by a ten megaton rocket booster. I could swear my body came close enough to our moon's surface to reach out and pinch off a piece of that infamous green cheese.

The extreme effects of the potent, nicotine induced hallucinations had stimulated all of the senses, including my sense of smell.

Upon my approach of the moon, the aroma of lengthy aged cheese filled the air. As I hovered overhead, my degree of imagination lost all boundaries and my most prevalent thought was, *it really is made of green cheese. I can smell it all the way up here.*

After that initial revelation, my next thought was, *and let the adventure begin*. And did it ever!

As I approached our milky way, I was privy to inspect it from a bird's eye view. Making a clockwise observation of the system, I viewed all of the elemental details up close and personal.

There was Perseus Arm, our own Solar System, Cycnus Arm, Centaurus Arm, Sagittarius Arm, and the notorious Orion Arm.

It was an uphill battle resisting the gravitational force that held the galaxy together. But I managed to traverse the entire 225 million light year trip around the outer rim of our Milky Way with lightning speed.

The next spectacle on my Black Maria excursion was Andromeda, about 2.2 million light years away, and one and a half times larger than our own Milky Way. And its gravity packed a force that felt one and a half times stronger than the last galaxy. But I kept on trekking, and with more than 300 billion stars contained within that one stellar system alone, I made good use of the designer Ray Ban sunglasses that miraculously appeared in my pants pocket. And my space odyssey was not over yet. Not by a long shot.

At the core of our own local galaxy was the Virgo Cluster, dead center a Super cluster made up of many more galaxies. It was huge with thousands of different galaxies in all shapes and sizes. I couldn't believe my eyes. I was physically close enough to spit on some of the fantastic, intergalactic wonders I had read about during our studies of the universe in Mr. Taborn's science class.

Billions upon billions of stars, encompassing thousands upon thousands of unusual, multi-sized and shaped galaxies, including the Sombrero Galaxy, the Polar Ring Galaxy, and the Siamese Twin Galaxies, just to name a few, became my playing grounds. My utmost consideration was that I had Black Maria to thank for that unimaginable, truly unique space sojourn that had been granted to me free of charge.

I soared pass the disreputable, and not surprisingly huge, Black Hole, and witnessed the death and rebirth of millions of brightly illuminant stars.

I even discovered galaxies from the past, some billions of years old that were buried deeply within the evolutionary history of the universe.

Suddenly, I was thrust into the recent past. Then things really got crazy. I witnessed Mr. Armstrong's historic landing on the moon, while I took a skinny dip in the Sea of Tranquility. I watched him trek across our moon's lunar surface. I listened as he delivered that resounding, "One giant leap for mankind," oratory. And I could swear he looked up at me while I was suspended in mid air, gave me a wink, and waved a friendly 'so long' before I was propelled into another enormous cluster of unknown galaxies.

Before my hellacious travels through those unfamiliar galaxies came to an end, I stumbled upon a hundred more immense Black Holes and uncovered a half dozen unknown planets yet to be discovered by modern man.

Then, suddenly, just as swiftly as my out-of-this-world journey had begun, it was now coming to a screeching end. My body was shifted into reverse. I plummeted downward, head first, at a thousand miles an hour, back into the earth's atmosphere.

All of the familiar sights came back into focus; the vast mountains, the seven seas, the country landscape, and the verdant fields that I'd roamed so freely. Before long I could see our house, the porch, and the quilt, from which my horrendous quest had started.

I felt somewhat like Humpty Dumpty must have felt when he was tumbling off that wall, anticipating the sound of a deafening splash, as I splattered all over the porch like an egg being dropped on cold, hard concrete. But, to my most pleasant surprise and delight, the touchdown was as cushioned as landing on a bed of cotton. And as I opened my eyes to the touch of Ma's hand and the summoning of her comforting voice saying, "Wake up, son. You been sleep all afternoon," I grasped one very important reality; there really is no place like home. Curiosity probably did kill the cat. And that Ma would have indeed whipped me back to sobriety if she knew just how far I'd travelled from that spot on the porch where I lay plastered, face down on the cement, and how it came to be.

I've heard her say too many times, "What you don't know can't hurt you." And who was I to dispute Mama's word?

So, up until this day, the secret of my unauthorized travels into inner and outer space, had remained sealed safely between the lips of this unwieldy space cadet, and my unforeseen, aero-space comrade, one Neil L. Armstrong, and God. What can I say but, "Mum's was the word," and "Yo, Neil, What's up? We know something they don't!"

HO DOWN SHOW DOWN

"Hey, Jimmy Lee, when y'all gon' git this here band set up so we can get this party started?" Julia Jackson, wearing that steamy ruby red lipstick and her hot pressed hair pinned up in a French roll, yelled out to Jimmy Jones. "I'm ready to shake my shimmy. I been waitin' all summer long for this here Ho Down. Git to strummin' that there guitar. We ain't payin' y'all to stand 'round an' do nothin'."

"Now, hold yo' horses, gal. We ain't warmed up yet. You know you can't rush perfection," Jimmy Lee boasted, flashing his pearly white teeth and his teasing brown complexion, as he rubbed back his processed hair with his right hand. "Just hold on. We gon' give you yo' money's worth an' then some. Don't you fret none 'bout that. We aims to please. They don't call me Jimmy 'Guitar' Jones for nothin'," Jimmy Lee bragged even more, while he set up his sound system. He inserted the cords running from the bottom of his steel guitar into the four foot tall speakers which amplified every note he strummed with the help of his pearl guitar pick.

If I could bring back my personal version of the 'Good Ol' Days', I'd be living on Hoke Journigans' tenant farm on Peter Gill road, at Route 1 Box 40-B.

I'd be romping around in that two-story, wood-frame house, sitting on top a hill, in the middle of a curve, framed by wild roses, nestled in a grove of stately pines and fifty foot tall pecan trees.

Back in those days, life was simple and unstressed. Neighbors were friendly and neighborly. We were just plain folk . . . salt of the earth.

I practically grew up in the cotton patch. I learned some of life's most valuable lessons straddling the rows between those tall, green stalks. I'd be snatching balls of cotton with both hands, from the middle of those razor sharp burrs and cramming them into that gunny sack tied around my waist that I dragged behind me. Or handing leaves to four middle-aged women, with lightning fast hands at the tobacco barn. And I had the most fun of my entire life.

There were many definition of 'fun' in those days. Fun was playing a game of soft ball in that sand lot in front of the house. Or ducking behind tall evergreens, dodging a huge ball hurled in the air at fifty miles an hour.

But the 'crème de la crème' of all the fun events I experienced during those good ol' days, was sampling a country smorgasbord of down home cooking at the annual Ho Down.

We sharecropped on a farm that was more than five-hundred combined acres of tobacco, wheat, cotton, corn and soybean. I saw it as an endless roadway into the wild, blue yonder. And I joyously explored every acre like a free-range chicken. My scope of curiosity and natural sense of wanderlust instilled in me a total sense of unrestraint . . . and I exercised those feelings daily to the fullest extent.

I was a wayward child by nature. I had more fun roaming around in the woods alone, than I ever had playing with the other children on the farm . . . which I did very little of. And on those rare occasions when I did participate in whatever games were played, or activity in motion, I was, without a doubt, going to be the boss.

I'd habitually play mean tricks on the other kids because I simply did not want to be bothered. That was my way of convincing them to leave me the heck alone. I thought they were all country heathens and didn't want to waste my time on them. So I always had more fun doing things on my own and in my own way.

Even when we'd be at that big tobacco barn, down the hill from our house, partying all night long at one of the big Ho Downs. I'd perch myself on that big pale rock we called 'white top', that rose two feet out of the ground, to sit down and gobble up the food I'd stacked four inches high on my plate. Then I just waited for the entertainment to begin, watching the rest of the gang get sloppy drunk and make pure divine fools of themselves.

Jimmy Lee and the band were finally warmed up, and Millie Brown strutted up to the mike, sporting a midnight blue midi dress and a matching box shaped feather hat. She started wailing out one of her original songs she titled, "**Cott'n Pickin' Blues**":

> *I ain't sleep at all last night,*
> *'Cause I spent all night long searchin' for my man.*
> *The broke devil had to been hidin''*
> *an' that's all right,*
> *'Cause I done found me another man.*
> *An' I ain't gon' be singin' no mo' of these Cotton Pickin' Blues.*

Becca Green, profiling a lime green straw hat that shadowed the dimples on her chubby cheeks, poised her hands on her full hips to steady herself. She hollered out from the front of the barn, "Got some fried fish sammiches for sale, a dollar a piece. Got chicken breast sammiches for a dollar fifty each."

Cally Dunston, leaned back, walked up to the checkered tablecloth that matched the red and white scarf tied around her head, and announced, "I got hamburgers, hotdogs an' soda pop, just a dollar twenty five each wit' a drink. If you want sumthin' stronger, that be at the bar, left side of the barn."

That was Bo Ellis' cue, flaunting his olive green pinstripe suit and Stetson hat, to announce his inventory of spirits. "You want somethin' HIGH OCTANE? Well I got some Blackberry wine, some Plum wine, some Peach Brandy, an' some two month old, White Lightnin', all homemade of course. Who wants the first sample?"

Wade Finch, in his denim suit and matching shirt, stepped up to the bar. "My mouth is dryer than a corn field in a drought," he said. "Gimme a fifty cent shot of that there White Lightnin'. I don't want none of that weak stuff. This here's a man," he announced, patting his chest with his hands. "I needs me a man's drink!" He looked back at Andy Jackson and asked, "Hey, Andy, you man 'nough to handle a shot of this here White Lightnin?"

"Ahh, shucks, man!" Andy bragged, in his three piece, royal blue vested suit. "I growed up on this here stuff. Drunk it in my milk bottle when I was a baby."

They both fell out laughing.

Andy reached into his right pocket and took out a crumpled up dollar bill and handed it to Bo.

"Hell! Give me two fifty cent shots, Bo. One ain't gon' be 'nough."

Bo looked up at Andy and said, "Don't know if I oughta give you a double shot at one time."

"Shoot! That ain't no big thang. You know I can drank anybody in this county under the table. Lemme have it!"

"Look, man," Bo continued with a grin, "This stuff is 170 proof. I'm tryin' to save lives here. This stuff strong 'nough to burn a blood blister on shoe leather."

"I know," Andy rattled on, "But you forgot my head is built from concrete, my heart is made outta lead, an' my stomach is pure galvanized steel. Now gimmee a double shot of that there White Lightning!"

Bo gave in, followed Andy's instructions and filled up the shot glass and handed it to him.

Andy turned the glass up to his mouth, took one big gulp, and lowered the glass, making a face that would scare the pure heck out of the devil. Then he made a loud growling noise, shook his head twice, and ordered another shot.

By the time Andy was through gulping down his third shot, he'd worked up the nerve to take to the dance circle. He reached out and grabbed Mabel Manson's hand, wrapped his right arm around her full waist, and started slow dragging across the yard while Millie swooned the crowd singing ,

> *Rock me baby 'til the sun comes up*
> *Get down an' dirty an' do the Huckle Buck*
> *Squeeze me, tease me*
> *Don't let me go*
> *Rock me honey, 'til*
> *I can't stand one bit mo' . . .*

The cussing coming from the other side of the barn was a deserving distraction from Andy's attempts to imitate the art of dancing. That only meant one thing; the crap game was in under way. I heard my daddy's voice yell out, "You liver-lipped Son- of- a-B---h! You know you throwed a 'leven!"

The next voice I hear is Cousin Bruce Harris saying, "Naw, I didn't, you no-teeth mutha . . .! You know I throwed a seven. Give me my doggone money or I'm gon' gut you like a hawg!"

Then, out came the switch blade; Black folks, white folks, young folks and old, scattered like flies being chased by a can of Black Flag bug spray.

All the party goers out on the yard that had been trying to show off the Slop, the Twist, the Cool Jerk, and the Mash Potato, started doing a new dance called Running for Cover.

Poor Jake Hunter, with his weak left leg from childhood Polio, disappeared from my sight after somebody ran him down, and the rest of the crowd just stampeded over his body like a herd of spooked cattle. Melvin Hunt reached down and grabbed him by the shirt collar and dragged him along without even slowing down his pace.

I didn't move from my spot at the edge of the road. I'm far enough from all of the excitement to be safely out of harm's way, and enjoy some of the best free entertainment of my young life; watching those country morons pound on each other like cavemen fighting for a fresh cut of dinosaur meat..

And the fun still wasn't over. Not 'til Pinto Brown, wearing denim coveralls, the only underdressed person at the Ho Down, beat somebody to a pulp. And that night it was poor, unlucky Romeo (RJ) Johnson.

I heard Pinto's voice rumbling from the far side of the barn, "Ahh, naw you ain't!"

I looked up just in time to see him jump up, flip the card table over on the ground, and reach for Romeo, who stumbled backwards, trying not to be hit by the tumbling table. "You puny, lil card cheat! Drop that ace from under yo' sleeve!"

Romeo swore, "Ain't no card up my sleeve."

"You a lyin' lil puny card cheat! Ain't but four aces in a deck of cards. How come there's two aces of spades, one ace of diamonds, an' one ace of clubs on the table? What happened to the ace of hearts? Wherever t'is, that's gon' make five Aces. I never see'd no deck of cards wit' five aces."

Pinto looked at the other players "Y'all ever see'd a deck of cards wit' five aces?"

Everybody shook their heads, and answered at the same time, "Not me."

Romeo turned to run, but Pinto grabbed the back of his shirt and dragged him across the overturned table.

"I'm gon' teach you a lesson you puny lil card cheat!"

All of a sudden, Romeo must be suffering from a bout of temporary insanity, because he got bold enough to stand up to Pinto. "I ain't scared of you, you big, black, fat lipped, cup cake. You just a big bag of hot air! You don't scare me none. An', yea, I won yo' money an' you ain't gittin' it back. If you want it back, you gon' have to come 'cross this table an' take it, you big, black, fat lipped, cup cake!"

Before I knew it, I heard myself say, "Ahh, shoot! Romeo done lost his mind 'cause that's just what Pinto gon' do!"

Pinto was stark, raving mad. I half expected to see smoke snorting from his nostrils. Although, he stood six foot six, and weighed in at two hundred thirty pounds, and Romeo weighed only a hundred and twenty pounds soaking wet, giving Pinto more than a hundred pound advantage over him, Romeo was not backing down.

Pinto wrapped his huge, black hands around Romeo's throat and lifted him clean off the ground. Pinto was so thick, all I could see was poor Romeo's feet kicking in the air. Then he shifted his position exposing Romeo's backside. I noticed Romeo's tan khaki pants starting to look wet. Then a stream of fluid came trickling down his legs and dripped onto the ground. Pinto was, literally, choking the pee out of Romeo.

Marshall Thomas rushed over to Pinto and started trying to pry his hands from around Romeo's neck. When Marshall was finally able to free Romeo from the grips of Pinto's big, merciless hands, Romeo's limp body just dropped to the ground like a wet noodle. His pupils were rolled back in his head and all you could see were the whites of his eyes.

Ralph Brown ran over and checked for a pulse to see if Romeo was breathing and gave the 'thumbs up' to the crowd, so everybody would know he was still amongst the living.

Hoke Journigan pulled up on his green 1952, Ford pickup just in time to see Romeo hit the ground. He walked over to Pinto, yelling and shaking that old walking stick in Pinto's face. "Great day'n the mornin', man, you done pret' near killed the boy! You done squeezed the pee right out o' the po' devil! I got a good mind to git my squirrel rifle an' fill yo' black behind wit' buck shots, an' shoot yo' tail right off this spot. Go on back to Miss'ssippi where you come from. You good for nothin' but trouble. Git off my place an' stay off!"

I noticed Pinto starting to make a fist and raise his right hand like he was about to introduce Hoke to some black skin. Ol' Hoke nearly broke his neck when he tripped over his own feet and ended up crawling on hands and knees across that hard ground, scrambling back to his pickup. I'm blinded for a second by all the dust the tires on that ol' truck kicks back when Hoke takes off down Peter Gill Road, gripping the steering wheel with both hands.

Bo and Marshall sat Romeo up and Mabel dipped a towel into the tub of melting ice and gently patted Romeo's face with the icy-cold cloth, which stunned him out of the near coma from being choked half to death.

Jake Scott lead Pinto back under the barn shed where Bo stood. The three men stood there conversing when Jake patted Pinto on the back and I heard Jimmy Lee say, "That's the man thang to do, Pinto. We all buddies here, man. Don't let a silly squabble end a life-time friendship."

Pint nodded his head, walked over to Romeo and offered a hand to lift him off the ground. Then he let his hand go as Romeo steadied himself, and extended his hand again offering to shake and settle their differences.

The two shook hands again and gave each other a manly hug. Then Pinto wrapped his right arm around Romeo's back, patted him on the right shoulder, and moved forward toward the bar, causing Romeo to do the same. He looked over at Romeo and said, "Buy you a drink for old times?"

Romeo nodded his head and answered, "Why not? For old times."

As they got closer to the bar, Pinto reached into his left pocket, pulled out a dollar bill, and slapped it down on the bar. He looked up at Bo, who had repositioned himself behind the bar, and ordered, as he pointed to Romeo, "A drink for my friend here. An' one for me," and watched as Bo filled the two glasses to the rim.

They both lifted the shot glasses into the air and touched the tops together, creating a jingling sound, and toasted, "To the good times. An' to good friends."

One hour later things had settled down. Bo started packing up all the shot glasses, the empty wine and liquor bottles, and politely announced, "The bar is now closed; an' to all, a good night."

As the rest of the gang headed home in all directions, Romeo stayed to help Bo clean up. Pinto headed up the path behind the strip house past the grain silos. Unaware that Hoke was dead set on making him pay for humiliating him in front of all of his tenants, Pinto strutted up the path humming to himself, which is why he did not hear the three men coming up behind him.

The first blow on the back of the head rendered him defenseless. After that, the beat down was just pure, unadulterated brutality. All Pinto could do was try and block the blows with his hands, as the hooded thugs took turns pounding on his body with the solid wood baseball bats.

Romeo came upon the scene just short of too late and yelled out to the three assailants, "Hey! Git off of him!" He picked up a huge rock and hurled it in the air, hitting one of the men in the temple. Blood stained the white hood covering his face, as the other two grabbed hold of his arms and practically dragged him up the path.

Romeo ran to Pinto's side. Blood covered most of his face. Several of his ribs protruded through his skin as he lay gasping for breath. His left eye was completely closed. And he had soiled his pants as a result of the excruciating pain he'd had to endure.

Pinto's vision was so blurred he did not recognize the person bending down beside him, until Romeo spoke.

"Lawd hammercy, man, who done this to you?"

Pinto tried to speak, but did not have the breath to do so.

Romeo offered to run back to the barn and try and catch Bo before he left, but Pinto would not let go of the solid grip he had on Romeo's arm.

A few moments later, the circulation started to return to Romeo's hand. The grip was released. Pinto's hands fell to his side as the last breath of life left his body.

At that moment, the thin, former weakling known as Romeo Johnson, became a modern day Hercules. He scooped Pinto up in his arms and headed back to the barn.

Bo was about to pull off in his powder blue, 1952 T-Bird, when Romeo yelled, "Stop, Bo! I need help!"

Bo jammed on the breaks and jumped from the car when he saw little Romeo carrying great big Pinto in his arms like a baby.

Romeo gently laid Pinto's body on the ground in front of the barn door.

Bo ran over but promptly looked away upon seeing Pinto's bloody body sprawled out on the ground.

"What the hell happened, Romeo?" Bo asked, with a trembling voice.

"On my way up the path I see'd three men wearin' hoods beatin' Pinto wit' baseball bats. I hollered out at 'em, an' racked one of 'em up side the head wit' a rock. Bust that skull wide open. Last I see'd of him, they was pret' near draggin' him up the path. I was too late to do anythang for Pinto, but I sure drawed blood from one of them bulldozers."

Bo regained his nerves and reached down to check Pinto's wrist for a pulse. There was none. He was gone.

The two of them managed to lift Pinto into the back seat of Bo's car and transported him to the colored hospital where he was pronounced dead on arrival.

Pinto had no known family or life insurance so Wake Jarvis, who owned the farm where Pinto worked, had his body cremated and gave the ashes to Romeo to do with them as he pleased.

The next day, Bo, Romeo, and the other sharecroppers on the Journigan farm, spread Pinto's ashes over Hoke's vegetable garden, asking God to let him choke on every bite of food he ate from that spot.

Ol' Hoke never got wind of the primal ritual that took place in his garden that day.

When the leaves changed color and started falling off the trees, Hoke's health started to fail. Every morsel of food that went down his throat, came spurting back up like crude, gushing from the pipes of an oil well. He was later diagnosed with stage IV stomach cancer, endured twelve months of severe abdominal pain and suffering, and died on the one-year anniversary of Pinto's murder.

Like the old folks 'roun' here like to say," Ain't no law south of the Mason-Dixon Line for culud folks. But that Higher Justice will always prevail. It's just a matter of time!"

CAT RUN

    Bertha struts her short, stocky body into our old fashioned kitchen, with hands in her apron pockets and orders, "Robert Willis Carroll, git up from that table this minute! You need to be headin' o'er to Wiley's place right now. He be waitin' for you to come an' help do his chores. I swear! You gon' wipe all the flowers off my plate soppin' that gravy wit' them biscuits!"

    "Can't help it, Bertha. Nobody can cook up a pan of rabbit an' gravy like you can."

    "That's fine an' good, but you need to be on yo' way. 'Fo' you know it, the sun'll be goin' down."

    "Yes, Ma'am, Miss Bertha. I be on my way right now."

    My Bertha is the sweetest thing on Earth. But she don't take no mess, especially from me. When she says, 'jump', I ask, "How high?"

    For the past six years, I been going over to my friend, Wiley Cox's house to do chores around his place. He lost his left leg, up to the knee, in the big war in 1918.

Wiley is a proud man, and it took some doing for him to handle that he can't do all the things he used to do and accept help, even from me, his life time friend. He thinks it's a burden for me to come over and do all them chores after working for ten or more hours in the field, but it's the proudest thing I do most days. In my eyes, he's the all-American hero who came just short of giving it all up fighting for his country, so nothing I do for him could be too much.

My Christian name is Robert Willis Carroll. But close friends call me 'Cut', cause in my younger, wilder days, if you crossed me, I'd cut you. Thank the Good Lord I've changed, but the name stuck.

My thoughts of Wiley get broken by a voice calling from down the way. It's another friend, Ernest (Hawk) Hawkins.

"Hey, Cut, hold up a minute," Hawk says. "Got somethin' I want you to see."

Hawk pulls the buckboard right in front of me, blocking my path, so there's nothing I can do but stop and have a look see. I gotta stand on my tip-toes to see over the side of the wagon. I almost fall backwards. There, stretched out the whole length of the wagon, is the biggest male cougar I ever did see.

"Lawdy, Miss Clawdy! Hawk, I swear, that's the biggest cat anybody's brung down yet. That rascal's gotta be eight feet long from his nose to the tip of his tail."

"At least," Hawk agrees. "An' he's gotta be pretty doggone strong to boot, to brang down my best breedin' bull. That devil hit Milt Jones' place last night, too. Took down half of his chickens an' four hawgs. I lit out trackin' him b'fo daylight an' I won't comin' home 'til he was gone for good. I know there's plenty mo' of 'em left out there, but this here fella won't be doin' no mo' killin'."

"What you brang him down wit'? I ask.

Hawk reaches under the wagon seat and pulls out a powerful looking gun.

"This here's my Winchester thirty odd six. It's got a K-4 scope for some real fast shootin'. An' it still won't easy killin' this big cat. Took three shots to bring him down."

"What you gon' do wit' him?" I ask, out of curiosity.

Hawk boasts real proud, "This fella gon' stand b'side the fireplace in my front room. Gonna take him o'er to Scarborough's Taxidermy directly an' let him stuff an' paste him onto one of them cedar slabs so he can stand guard o'er the house."

"At this size, even dead, he makes a pretty good watch dog," I joke.

We both have to laugh.

"You on yo' way to Wiley's place?" Hawk asks.

"Yea, I'm goin' over to pay him a little visit an' see what chores need to be done, an' head on back to the cut (home)."

"Give Wiley my regards an' tell him I'll be seein' him soon, okay?"

"I'll do that. Be seein' you."

We both tip our hats and wave good-bye.

Hawk clicks his teeth, cracks the reins over the mules' backs, and yells, "Giddy up." The wagon jerks off and heads down the path towards his log cabin, about a mile pass the end of the corn field. I head to Wiley's place.

It's almost sun down before I finish mauling the pile of wood I'd been chopping on the side of Wiley's house.

When Wiley come home from the war, I sort of took it upon myself to be his helping hand.

Every evening, when I leave Wiley's house, there's a fresh pile of wood beside the door on his front porch. I know that Wiley can manage to hop to the front porch and bring in a few sticks of wood at a time, to keep his fire going through the night if he needs to. So I feel okay leaving him alone.

Other neighbors volunteer to help out, too.

Ms. Maybelle Evans makes sure Wiley has at least one hot meal a day. Before she enters the house she lets Wiley know she's there and yells out "Yooh! Whoo!, Wiley, you decent.

Wiley answers "Jes barely, but come in anyhow. Glad for de company."

She walks in, greets the two of us, and tells Wiley what's in the wicker basket swinging from her arm. "I brought you some fried chicken, some fresh collard greens, some tater salad, some hot biscuits, an' some blackberry cobbler. Hope you good an' hungry."

Wiley answers "I sho' is."

When Wiley wobbles into the kitchen to wash his hands, Miss Evans places the small table that sits under the window, by the side of the bed. She takes the red and white checkered cloth from the basket, snaps it once in the air to remove any wrinkles, and spread it over the table, along with a spoon, knife, fork, and napkin.

Wiley sits back down and says the blessings, followed by 'Amen.' Both Miss Evans and I say 'Amen', too.

While Wiley enjoys the food, Miss Evans straightens up the house. When Wiley is done eating, she washes the plate in the dish pan on the kitchen table, puts the card table back under the front window, and makes her excuses for not staying longer. "I hate to rush but I promised Molly Jones I'd fix some food to take over to the Ramsey's place for the 'settin' up'. It sure was a shock how Pete just fell dead like that in the tobacco field yestiddy. Folks say he had a heat stroke. I say he just had one drink too many of that white lightnin' he gits from Larry Cousins, but you didn't hear it from me."

We all laugh and Miss Evans steps out onto the front porch and promises, "I'll be back tomorrow, Wiley. Picked me some fresh string beans, an' dug up me some new baby potatoes, early this mornin, so I'll bring you some for lunch tomorrow, okay?"

"Yes, Ma'am, I'll be lookin' forward to it. I thank you for all you do."

"I know you do" she replied. And you're very welcome."

She closes the door and her footsteps slowly fade off into the distance.

J. T. Bowling is another neighbor who makes sure Wiley's hogs and chickens get fed each day. Most days Wiley doesn't know he's around until he call out, "Here, chick, chick, chick!" as he scatters hands full of corn and grain out on the yard for the chickens to peck.

Next he hears him sing out, "Suey! Suey!" He looks out the windows to see J.T. spreading slop over the trough in the pig pen. J.T. waves from across the yard, completes the chores at hand, and is gone in a flash, knowing all the while that Wiley appreciates everything he does.

Even the mercantile, T. K. Whitmore, delivers a few groceries every week when he makes deliveries to other folks in the area in his Studebaker wagon. He always tells Wiley, "Don't worry 'bout the money."

He's always in a hurry, so he puts the groceries in the cupboard in the kitchen, walks over to shake Wiley's hand, then mine, and is back out the door in a few minutes, always promising, "I'll be back next week."

And, so far, he's kept his word.

Each day, after I finish the chores, I feel obliged to sit a spell and chew the fat with Wiley. The subject is always the same, my wife, Bertha, his late wife, Maxine, the burning sensation of the bullets penetrating his flesh to the bones, the surgery amputating his leg, his willingness to do it all over again if necessary, and the Purple Heart given to him by President Woodrow Wilson.

Our visits always end with Wiley thanking me for all I do for him and for being his friend. My response is always the same, "An' you know I'll always be, long as the Good Lawd keeps breath in my body."

Then he reaches into his pants pocket, pulls out the gold watch the U.S. Army gave him, flips open the cover and says, "Gittin' close to seven o'clock. These late summer days can still be a bit long, but the sun be goin' down soon. Think you betta be gittin' on back to the 'cut', don't you, Cut?"

We both laugh at the joke.

"Guess t'is," I answer.

Before I leave I always make sure everything is locked up and tell Wiley to, "Sleep tight and remember, tomorrow is a brand new day."

When I first started the shortcut through the woods from my house to Wiley's place, there was nothing but thick patches of grass along the way. Now the route to Wiley's place is a clear path of beat down red sod, after six years of daily round trips from my house to his.

Most days, I'm so wrapped up in my thinking, the trip to Wiley's house is over before I know it. The thickets are so deep in some spots along the path, I can't see what's on the other side of them. And there's many a days when I sense there's something behind them thickets that can clearly see me. Sometimes the feeling is so strong, it feels like eyes be staring me down so hard, they look right through me. There's even been times when I felt that something was so close, I could hear a deep purring in my ears. And that's the times when I pick up the pace and waste no time getting to where I'm going.

Them woods is full of high timbers as far as yo' eyes can see. There's also a whole passel of wild animals that prowl them woods from dusk 'til dawn. And any unlucky soul who happens to cross they path at night, could be the next victim of they devil nature and end up being mauled to death, or clawed into lil pieces. I got no idea that tonight I could be one of them victims.

I was working real hard in a small tobacco field next to the irrigation pond, just whistling to myself, trying to finish the last priming, and get it off to the market. I happen to look up at the sky and notice the sun's starting to go down.

I yell out loud to myself, "I need to head off to Wiley's place to take care of his chores." I start stepping and don't stop 'til I see Wiley's two-room cabin at the clearing. My mind is running like a 'coon bein' chased by a hound dog, and I start talkin' to myself again. "I ain't gittin' caught in these here woods after dark. I gotta git these chores done for Wiley an' git back home lickety split."

I done sat on my porch many a nights and listened to them big cats growling and prowling the woods in the dark of night, and I was glad to be one step from the inside of my house.

This evening won't be the case.

I cut the pile of wood in a hurry, stack it against the front door, come inside and visit with Wiley for a spell, do the other chores, and make sure the place is locked up before I head home.

Wiley is more than a little worried 'cause the sun is already set and it's getting too close to dark for me to make it home before every ray of daylight is completely gone.

"You gon' be alright, Cut?" Wiley asks. "It's mighty close to dark. You gotta run all the way to clear them woods 'fo all the light is gone. I'm a lil bit scared for you. You shouldn't of come this late to see 'bout me. I know you been tryin' to finish primin' that field off Grissom Farm Road. I woulda been alright 'til tomorrow."

"Don't you worry 'bout me, Wiley. You kno' I'll be okay. So don't you fret none. I'll see you tomorrow. Sleep well tonight. An' remember, tomorrow's a brand new day."

I smile at Wiley, leave the house in a hurry, and run across the yard towards the woods. I can't remember ever feeling so scared going through the woods. I try to ease my nerves and start singing one of my favorite gospel songs:

Thank You, Lawd, for savin' my soul
Thank You, Lawd, for makin' me whole
Thank You, Lawd, for givin' to me
Thy great salvation, so right an' free. . .

Before the last note rolls off my tongue, I hear the chilling, shrieking growl of the cougar and know, before the sound clears the cat's throat, it's hot on somebody's trail. When I turn and look behind me, and the critter come into view, it's pretty clear that the beast is hot on my trail.

I make a mad run towards home. I remember something I used to hear my pappy say . . . that when a big cat is chasing its prey, the dumb animal will stop, and attack whatever is in its path, whether it be living or dead. There was nothing in his path but me, and nothin' I could think of to put in his path but the clothes on my back, so, I start taking off my clothes, one piece at a time.

Six days every week, except on Sunday, I wear bib overalls, a blue, red, or green plaid shirt, a' old Stetson hat, and a pair of brown, Broke-Iron boots, a war keepsake from Wiley. (People call 'em Broke-Iron boots 'cause of the steel in the toe.)

When I look back again, the cat is dead on my trail. The hair on the back of his neck is standing straight up. Every one of his razor-sharp teeth are showing. All I can think of is to run like a rabbit in a briar patch. When I look back a third time, he's gaining on me like nobody's business. I know I gotta do something or I'm cat food for sure. I start ripping off clothes like a crazy man.

First I take off my Stetson hat and throw it on the ground. Sure enough, he stops and rips it to shreds.

Next, I take off my shirt. Just slide the straps off my shoulders and yank it from under my dungarees. That dumb cat stops and rips it to pieces, too.

I don't even take the time to unbuckle the straps on my bibs. I just try to step out of them.

The next thing I know, I'm flat on the ground when I get my feet tangled in the legs and hit the dirt hard as a rock.

It only takes me a second to get back on my feet, but that cat's running so fast, by the time I'm done stepping out of them dungarees, and get into a good running pace again, that cougar's so close on my tail, I can feel his hot breath on the back of my heels.

The only way I get to put distance between us is 'cause he stops to tear into them dungarees. But that don't take more than a minute, and he's hot on my trail again. All I have left to shed is my long johns and my Broke-Iron boots. I figure it'll take him a little longer to tear into them boots and that'll give me enough leeway to get home by the time he's done ripping them to pieces, so I step out of them boots without even unlacing them. Sure enough, he pounces on them boots like live prey. He picks them up in his mouth, shaking them back and forth, gnawing and clawing until there's nothing left but big shreds of leather.

Lawdy! Lawdy! I've never been so glad to see home in my whole life, as I turn the corner of the corn field and shift my run into overdrive. I'm running so fast I can hear my heart beating in my ears like a talking African drum. It's pounding hard against the walls of my chest. I think it's gonna break right through the skin. I'm huffing and puffing like a man trying to get air in a corked jug. My arms are moving like the oars on a row boat fighting white water. My head's laid back so far, trying to push myself forward, I feel like an owl with his face turned around backwards. My chest is stuck out so far, I must look like a rooster strutting around the barn yard. And the wind swooshing past my face is so strong, the flapping of my lips sound like a piece of cardboard caught in a bicycle spoke.

Looks like the harder I run, the farther the house moves away. When I get close enough for somebody inside the house to hear me, I start hollering to the top of my lungs, "Open the door! Open the door!"

I see the door fly open.

When I reach the front porch, I hear myself saying "Ain't 'nough time to clear all them steps. I gotta make it one step from here to the door." So I stretch my legs out as far as they can go to make one giant hop onto the porch and one long, stretched out step across the porch to the front door.

Before I completely clear the threshold, I yell, "Shut the door! Shut the door!"

I hear the door slam behind me. I don't know who did it and don't care. All I care about is that the door is between me and that cat. He was so set on tearing into my hide, he rams, head first, into the door and pret near knocks the sense out of hisself.

This is about the funniest and the scariest thing we ever seen, watching that cat stagger off the porch and wobble back up that path, mad as the devil cause he didn't git to draw my blood.

I stand in the middle of the floor shaking. The goose bumps on my flesh make my arms look like chicken skin. My eyes are set on all my children standing in front of me.

My voice trembles when I turn to Bertha, and say, "I gotta go after him, Bertha, or I won't ever feel t'is safe for 'em to walk that path ag'in."

Bertha agrees, and says, "Do what you gotta do, Cut."

I go to my room and put on another pair of boots, shirt, and dungarees. I come back into the front room and take my full choke 12-gauge shotgun from the rack over the fireplace. I grab a box of shells off the mantle, load the gun, and put the rest of the box in my pocket. I kiss Bertha and say, "Keep my supper warm, okay. I won't be long."

She nods, "Okay."

The Lord must really be on my side, 'cause soon as the daylight left, the full moon wasted no time lighting up the whole countryside so good, it looked like the sun never set. I lit out trailing that cougar with my mind set on bringing back his dead carcass to set my family's mind at ease that the path was safe to walk again. I didn't have to trail for long. Soon as I turned the corner, there he was, in plain sight, tearing into what was left of them boots. He got my scent right away and his attention shifted to me, live prey, real quick.

He was no more than 100 yards away when he bolted in my direction. I cock the shotgun and aim, counting down, out loud, the yards he covered with each leap, "90, 80, 70, 60, 50, 40, 30, 20," until he was in close enough range for me to take him down with one shot.

When I'm sure he's no more than 20 yards away, I brace myself and let him have it, just when he leaps into the air to pounce on me.

The shot goes straight through the heart and he drops to the ground making a loud thump. I ease over to the hundred and forty pound heap stretched out on the ground and poke it twice, real careful, with the barrel of the gun. It don't move.

I notice a real clear stain around his mouth. I bend down to take a closer look. Before I can catch myself, I say out loud, "That's dry blood. This here fella done killed somethin' not too long ago, an' here's the blood to prove it. Coulda been somebody's livestock. Coulda been Hawk's breedin' bull, or Milt Jones' hawgs an' chickens. Maybe Hawk killed the wrong cat. Can't be sure. But one thang I do know for sure, this big cat won't kill no mo."

I know I can't budge that big fella by myself, so I go back to the house and get three of my boys to go to the barn and tie together some cotton sheets. We go back up the path and roll the cat onto the sheets. The four of us grab hold of the front of the sheets and drag the cat to the house.

Everybody gotta take a look and poke it once or twice just to make sure it's really dead, before I lock it in the barn, with plans to give it to Hawk in the morning. That way, he'll have two big, stuffed cats guarding his house.

Now I gotta deal with my wife and children, and this coming home in my long Johns affair. When I walked through the back door from the barn, Bertha and all the children line up in front of me, with funny grins on they faces. My voice is cracking up when I say, "I know y'all gon' have a real good time makin' jokes 'bout the day yo' Papa come home wearin' nothin' but his long Johns. But, you know what, I'm so glad I got here in one piece, I'm gon' laugh right 'long wit' you."

Right now I feel the only thing in the world that's gon' make me feel better is somebody's warm arms around me, so I stretch 'em both way out to the sides and say, "Come give yo' papa a hug!"

All ten children come a running. So do Bertha.

We all join hands and give praise to the Almighty because we know that on this blessed night, I truly cheated death by the skin of my boots.

SOUTH PAW SAM

The day I met my, soon-to-be, long time friend, Samuel B. Hayes, he'd just jumped from a boxcar on an Eastern Seaboard Train and sprained his right ankle.

I was headed to Whites' Store to buy a pound of sugar for Ma to bake one of her Betty Crocker standard coconut cakes, when I spotted him straddling the steel track, clutching his leg, with a grimacing expression on his face. He looked to be around fifty, but I suspected he was a lot younger than he appeared. Being the curious child that I was, I asked, "What's the matter, Mister?"

He responded in the most crude, half legible version of the English language that I had ever heard. "Ah hurt mah leg w'en Ah jumped off de train," he said.

I didn't know this ragged stranger from Adam, but he put out 'good energy' so before I knew it, the words came gushing from my mouth, "Stay right there," I advised him. "I'll be right back. Gotta run to the store an' git some sugar. Then I'll take you home wit' me an' Ma will fix yo' leg right up. Okay?"

He just nodded his head and said, "Yessum."

I rushed to the store, bought the sugar, and returned to the spot where I'd left the man whose name I neglected to obtain.

He was still sitting there balancing his backside on the train railings. I reached down and took hold of his rough, calloused hand and helped him balance himself on his good foot. I casually asked him his name and he responded in an even cruder manner."Mah name be Samu'l B. Hayes. The 'B' stands for Beauregard, (which he did not pronounce anywhere close to the spelling.) He continued the introduction by saying, "Mah hoboin' friends calls me 'Southpaw Sam 'cause Ah plays mah guitar wit' mah left han'."

"Well then, Mr. Samu'l B. Hayes, my name is Begonia P. Monroe. But my friends call me Bee. And since I suspect we gon' be good friends real soon, I think I'd like to call you Southpaw Sam myself. That is, if it's okay with you?"

He flashed a friendly smile in my direction, revealing his poorly kept teeth and said, "Yessum, Ah likes dat jes' fine. Ah sho' do."

We strolled aimlessly down the path to our house, me with the bag of sugar swinging in one hand, and he, with an old Dobro Lap Steel Guitar, swinging from a frayed strap on his back.

I could not resist the urge to ask just what a 'hobo' was. And he proceeded to give me his own personal definition of the word.

"Ah don't rightly know whar de word 'hobo' come from, but we be a lonely bunch o' travelers, goin' wherever dey's work to be done. Once a hobo gits word dey's work somewhere 'long de rails, de news gits spread pretty fast, an' we take off to git our lil share o' de pickin's."

"Ain't you got no family, Southpaw Sam?" I asked.

"Don't rightly know. I growed up in de Logan House down in Valdosta, Georgia. Dat be a home for chillun wit' no Ma an' Pa. We called de folks who ran de home Ma and Pa Logan. Dey's de only folks dat evah seemed like family. Though dey treated me real good, Ah Left thar de day Ah was ol' 'nough to hold down a job, any kinda job, an' headed off to Chicago. Dey got a lot o' slaughter houses in Chicago ya know. Ah coulda stayed thar de rest o' mah life, but Ah got tired of smellin' like blood an' ol' guts. When Ah took my weekly bath, seemed like de harder Ah scrubbed mah skin, de mo' Ah stank. So, one day, Ah jes' up an' left. Caught me a freight train to Pennsylvania and never looked back. Dats' w'en Ah met some o' mah hoboin' buddies and we been ridin' de rails ever since. Sometimes we meet up on de way here an' thar, an' we talk 'bout whar we been an' whar we headed next. If thar's work on de way, we stop an' make a few honest dollars an' move on."

Continuing my nosey spree of none-of-my-business questions, I asked, "You carry that guitar wit' you everywhere you go, Southpaw Sam?"

"Yea, Ah do. Dis here is mah closest friend. Ah won dis guitar in a game o' poker in Baltimore, Maryland. Named her LouBelle after a soft, sweet smellin' gal Ah once had de pleasure to know down in New Orleans. You know, dey got some pretty, painted ladies in New Orleans. Full of spunk. Dey sho' know how to turn a man's head. Dat gal made me so crazy, Ah coulda swore she done put a spell on me. So I hopped a ride on de first train outta town, an' don't ever plan on goin' back."

He started laughing and continued, "Ah bet she done drove a passel o' men crazy since Ah high tailed it outta thar. But she sho' was a sweet thang."

"I'll bet you got a lot of stories to tell about the places you've been and the people you've met riding the rails," I said.

"I do dat. Some of 'em would probably curl up de hair on de back o' yo' neck. Ah had some good times an' thar was some bad times. But Ah do b'lieve thar been mo' o' de good dan de bad. An' de best thang tuh do is try an' make de best outta what ya got w'en ya gits it, an' keep on truckin'."

"Mr. Sam'ul B. Hayes," I replied, "You are what I would call a 'free spirit'."

"W'at's a 'free spirit'?" he asked.

"That's somebody who is free to come an' go as they please with nothin' to tie 'em down. Like you, Sam. And, by the way, do you mind if I call you

Sam? Southpaw Sam is just too long to have to say on a regular basis. And, besides, Sam just has a friendlier ring to it."

"Ya welcome tuh call me Sam if ya like. Ah been called 'Southpaw' so long it seemed like part of my real name."

"Well, Sam, you are a truly, divine 'free spirit'. Most folks probably envy you but they'd never admit it. They don't have that adventurous nature that you have. Most of us are just too bogged down wit' all the things we have like, cars, houses, clothes and stuff. But not you. You travel light. An' because of that, you can travel fast an' far. I'll bet all yo' earthy possessions are tied up in that sack on yo' shoulder, ain't they?"

"Yessum. Ah got all Ah need right here in dis ol' green duffle. Ya know, a hobo life ain't no bad way tuh live. Ya meet some real nice folks along the way. An' we hobos got our own way o' lettin' each other know if a place is friendly an' de folks livin' thar will stake ya a meal, or if you betta off stayin' on de train."

"You don't say!" I responded.

"Yea. We jes look for words an' signs carved on trees, or light poles, or anythang ya kin write on."

Still being nosey, I asked, "Can you read and write, Sam?"

"Yessum. Some. Ah kin write may name, read some o' de words in de Bible, and do mah sums. Ah kin count all de way to one hundred, an' kin count de devil outta some money. Can't nobody cheat me wit' no money. One time a fella tried to cheat me outta fifteen dollars w'en Ah bought some crackers an' sardines at dis country store. Ah give him a twenty dollar bill, three whole day's work, an' he swore Ah give him a five. Ah reached o'er dat counter an' took mah change right outta dat money drawer. He pulled out a switch blade and raked me 'cross de face. Ya kin still see de scar. But Ah sho' got mah money back."

The scar he referred to was a four-inch gash that had long been healed, but it covered the entire length of his left cheek. It was hardly visible without close observation, mostly concealed by the short, scruffy beard he wore and the weather-born signs of aging he displayed.

When we arrived at the house, I formally introduced Sam to Ma and the expression on her face read, *'another stray'* followed by a gentle smile

I informed her that he had sprained his ankle when he jumped off the train and I promised she'd bandage it up for him. She just looked at me again, and this time her expression read, *I need to bandage up your mouth 'cause that's the only way you'll keep it shut.* Then she flashed another warm smile in Sam's direction.

Since Ma could find a use for almost anything and didn't like the thought of wasting anything, she rarely threw anything away, even bed linens that were so full of holes you could sift flour through them. So she proceeded to the wardrobe and pulled out an old sheet, tore it into long strips, and carefully wrapped Sam's ankle and offered to run him a hot bath, which he graciously accepted.

The upper floor of our big farm house was just one huge room. It had three double beds, two dressers, and one big wardrobe to hold my two brothers' clothes. That was also the place for taking baths since we had no indoor plumbing. We filled two scrub tubs with water from the well, heated them on the old wood stove, lugged them up the stairs and emptied them into the large wash tub that we used for bathing as well as washing clothes on laundry day.

Meanwhile, Ma mixed all of the ingredients for the cake and placed the three pans of batter in the oven to bake.

When Sam reappeared in the kitchen, I swear his complexion was two shades lighter. His relatively good grade of salt and pepper hair had been washed and slicked back in rippled waves. His scruffy beard had been neatly shaven, making the lengthy scar on his left cheek more noticeable. The reeking odor that trailed behind him when he first arrived on the scene had been emancipated by the abrasive cleansing of the homemade lye soap. And the dregs of body sweat and particles of embedded dirt, that before had wafted over his entire anatomy, had equably settled on the bottom of that galvanized bathing vessel. Neither Ma nor I could believe our eyes. This Man, who less than an hour earlier was a vision of the most ragged and down-trodden vagrant on earth, had been transformed into a fine specimen of the male persuasion. His only article of clothing that could be salvaged was the vintage Cavanaugh hat, with a grey and black herringbone design. Although the one and a half inch coordinating hat band was so soiled and discolored from human sweat, it appeared to have been dipped in used motor oil, it was still such a classy accessory, it would have been a shame to toss it in the trash along with the other garments.

The oversized bibbed overalls that had been passed down from a neighbor to my brothers were a perfect fit for Sam's husky body. I don't know which articles of clothing he was more proud of, the overalls and secondhand long Johns, the grey wool jacket, or the blue flannel shirt that set off the entire get up. But he was proud indeed.

After the cake was iced to perfection, the table was set, and all of the neighborhood kids congregated to enjoy yet another of Ma's culinary delights, we all gathered at the elongated table and Sam offered the blessings.

"Our Father in Heaven, we thanks ya for dis meal dat we's 'bout tuh receive for de good o' our body an' soul. We thanks ya for de han's dat prepared it an' for mah new friend, Begonia. Help us tuh live each day as Ya will have us, Lawd. In de name of our Savior, Amen.'

I praised Sam for the wonderful sentiment and wasted no time digging into the homemade feast spread out before us. After we'd consumed more fried chicken, string beans and potatoes, corn and buttermilk biscuits than any non-gluttonous human being should, I asked Sam to play us a tune on his guitar. He eagerly obliged saying, "How 'bout 'Down By De River Side'?"

"Go for it, Sam," I urged, as he placed the guitar on his lap, secured the metal slide over the strings on the upper end of the guitars neck, and started strumming. The slide glided up and down the neck of the guitar, altering the pitch of each mellow tone resonated by the plucked strings. His words were enunciated less than perfect, but we all knew exactly what he was trying to articulate. By the time our impromptu gospel revival had ended, chanting such familiar tunes as "Amazing Grace," "The Old Rugged Cross," and "There's A Leak in This Ol' Building," we'd worked up enough appetite for a second slice of that coconut cake.

Sam hung around for another week, until a fellow trailblazer named, Sumpter Hall, showed up announcing there was work on a cotton plantation near Charleston, South Carolina. I asked Sam how the young fellow with a foot long ponytail, a 'Wyatt Earp style moustache, sun tanned complexion, and hazel green eyes, knew a fellow hobo was on the premises. That's when he schooled me about the hobo codes.

"'Member the day w'en we first met an' ya went tuh de store to buy dat sugah?" Well, while ya was gone, Ah took mah knife an' cut a hobo mark in dat tree by de millin' company whar de train stopped. T'was a square missin' de top line. Dat meant t'was safe tuh come here. But Ah also put two zigzaggin' lines, one on top o' de other, tuh let 'em know dey's barkin' dawg here, too." (The barking dog he referred to was our black Labrador Retriever we lovingly called, Shag.) He continued the mini course in hobo terminology and added, "If t'won't safe tuh come here, Ah woulda cut two lines goin' down from left tuh right. If Ah'd drawed a triangle wit' han's, dat meant de person here had a gun. An' one dat put de fear o' God in ev'ry hobo, is two han's locked together. Dat stand for handcuffs, an' any hobos seen in de area will be hauled off tuh jail."

The thought of Sam leaving left me feeling more than a little sad, because during the eight days that I'd known him, we had indeed become very good friends. But he eased my sorrow by assuring me he'd be back soon, and he was.

Our landlord's nephew, Tommy Edwards, had some knowledge of the ways of the hobo, and had left a sign on another tree near the milling company that there was work available. Every time the train stopped at the Dixieland Milling Company, I excitedly watched to see the six-foot-four silhouette darting behind the trees that lined the edge of the tracks, working its way towards the path leading to our house. After more than two weeks of disappointment, Sam reappeared. I met him half way up the path. He told me about the sign, and I expected the work he'd sought to be priming tobacco or picking cotton on the farm. But the work didn't involve farming at all. Tommy had been eyeing Sam since he'd first come on the scene. He figured Sam was gullible and desperate enough for money to go along with his illegal liquor operation and not make waves. Being the extremely naïve person that Sam was, Tommy had figured correctly.

Before Sam could reach the front yard, Tommy had intercepted his path and made him a financial offer that he could not resist, and he started work immediately, being Tommy's lookout man as well as his distilling assistant.

Weeks had passed before I became very suspicious of the extra cash Sam was spending on me and the other young people who frequented our house. Being a female in the early stages of puberty, and eager to keep in step with all the latest styles, I lashed onto every gifted dress or pair of new shoes that came my way. Then, one day, I decided to follow Sam down the path past that marvelous piece of black slate that protruded a few inches out of the ground. In the center of the three-foot wide rock was an intricate carving of a Native-American mother, carrying a papoose on her back.

As I approached the clearing, I expected to see a new field of young cotton or tobacco growing. But, instead, I found an industrial sized liquor still, concealed neatly inside a grove of pine and sycamore trees. Tommy was nowhere to be seen. But Sam was in clear sight, keeping check on the pressure gauges, making sure that the booze was brewed to perfection. I was fighting mad at the thought of Tommy taking advantage of my trusting friend. I walked up to Sam, took hold of his left arm, and led him back through the woods to our house. I patiently waited for Tommy to come past the house, knowing that he would eventually head to the site of his illegal past time and check on the condition of his financial gold mine. I didn't have to wait very long. When he approached the house, he noticed Sam and I standing in the yard. He stopped and we both walked out to the car to greet him. "You look almost human riding in yo' brand new, red, 1959 Oldsmobile '98' with that sharp, white convertible top, and them sporty whitewall tires," I said. "Now tell me this, how could a half illiterate fella, like yo'self, afford such a fine automobile as this?

He totally ignored me and tore right into Sam, asking, "Why de hell ain't you whar you s'posed tuh be, boy? I left you to watch my crop."

I immediately lit into him with a rebuttal and said, "You and I both know that you ain't growin' nothin' down in them woods but cultures to ferment that illegal liquor you distillin'. An' you ain't gon' use my friend no mo' to help you do it. An' if you try an' make him, I'm gon' put a lil bug in Sheriff Dudley's ear an' tell him all 'bout yo' lil distillin' operation."

Tommy was so mad, and the change in his skin tone was so drastic, he gave a whole new meaning to the phrase 'red neck'. And he came back with his own rebuttal, "Gal, don't you threaten me. I'll go all de way tuh de Supreme Court an' you still couldn't stop me from doin' w'at I'm doin'. 'Roun' dese here parts, yo' friend Sam's word wouldn't be worth snot. Who do you s'pose would take de word of a 'simple minded spook', like him, over mine? Nobody. So don't waste yo' time an' keep yo' bug to yo'self. Besides, Sheriff Dudley jes happens to be my best customer." He gave me an under eyed look, flashed a demonic grin in my direction, and said, "You better be glad I like you, gal. T'ain't ev'ry day I git tuh look at a pretty brown thang like you." Then he rolled the passenger window back up, sped off down the path, stopped the car just short of the woods, and disappeared among the trees.

I convinced Sam it was time for him to take a short leave, and he hitched a ride on the next train headed north.

A few weeks later, we had a visit from a hobo buddy of Sam's who told us the gruesome story of how his right pinkie finger had been cut off by a drunken bully outside a bar near Baltimore. The person, whose name was never disclosed, had noticed the guitar swinging on Sam's back and asked if he knew the words to the song "Stagger Lee", and Sam said he did, but added that he only sang gospel songs. When the drunk insisted that Sam sing the song anyway, and he refused, the person took out his switch blade and said, "Well, since you don't seem to have a reason to sing the blues, let me give you one." Then he grabbed hold of Sam's hand and whacked off the finger.

All I could see in my head, was the vision of that band of white-gold overlaying a yellow-gold base, of his late mother's 14K gold ring. It was the only thing he had to remind him of his mom, which was given to him after her body was dragged from the Santee River, where his father had dumped it the day he cut her throat from ear to ear.

Late in the summer, that same year, a middle-aged couple, the Collins, bought the ranch-style, green and white house at the end of the path, just short of the road. Mrs. Collins, a short, portly woman with snowy white hair and round rimmed glasses, was the perfect poster child for Mrs. Claus because she had an acute liking for the color red. In fact, most of her floor length dresses and floral aprons were mostly red with splatters of white, or black, or blue embedded in the design.

Mr. Collins, a retired science professor from Towson University, was strange in a major sort of way. He seemed to enjoy relishing over his formaldehyde specimen displayed throughout his one room basement, more than eating when he was hungry. The both of them became friendly right away, but I approached Professor Collins with more caution; I didn't like his energy. Even though he was cordial and seemed very down to earth, to be a smart college professor, he emitted an air of sinister magnitude that caused me discomfort when I was around him. Which is why I'd politely refused to oblige him each time he invited me to his basement lab to have a look at the multitude of well preserved embodiments that had migrated with him from Baltimore.

Finally, after his tenth invitation, I accepted and cautiously followed him into the blood curdling dungeon. To say it was spooky would be an understatement. The scene was scary, but awe inspiring. I had never, in my thirteen years, seen so many perfectly preserved specimens of infant hogs, cats, toads, and even one that I could have sworn was a real human baby. But, I asked no questions about the contents of his scientific inventory. Not even when my eyes became fixated on the brown pinkie finger floating weightlessly in a small mason jar, with a white-gold band overlaying a yellow-gold base on the 14K gold ring, that was snuggly wedged onto the finger. I may have thought it a rare coincidence had it not been for the familiar initials engraved on the top of the ring which read, SBH to LBH.

The look on his face said clearly that the content of that jar was his most prized possession. It was almost impossible for me to contain my anger when he bragged that he'd obtained it from a niggra who didn't know his place. My concealed rage mounted near out of control when he boasted even more that an auctioneer had offered him one hundred and seventy five dollars for the privilege of owning a piece of Southern Americana. He'd respectfully refused to part with that 'one-of-a-kind keepsake', as he called it. I called it a dirty, rotten shame, to myself, and promptly ended my tour of the cursed basement freak show. I ascended the stairs and pledged to never set foot on them again. And I kept my word.

That same day, a very sad, and disheartened Sam returned. We gathered in the back yard, and with much effort, I finally convinced Sam to play for us. The trump card was I had to agree to bring my color-coded player piano outside and accompany him with the keyboard. We started off singing "He's Got the Whole World in His Hands", and ended our outdoor impromptu non-tent revival with "How I Got Over."

After the incident with the finger in the jar of formaldehyde, someone had started paying very close attention to Professor Collins' daily routine, outside of his house. Halfway into that month, he came up missing and so did the jar containing the floating, ringed finger. The Sheriff and all of his four deputies looked day and night for more than a week, but there was no sign of Professor Collins, anywhere.

By the end of that same month, the smell surrounding the well was becoming more and more difficult to ignore. And then the buzzards started circling overhead. Mrs. Collins had complained about her sinus problems since the first day we met, so her sense of smell was more than a little compromised, and she continued drawing water from the well as usual.

Then Sheriff Dudley started getting complaints from nauseated citizens in close proximity to the Collins' home and came out to investigate. The putrid odor of the severely decomposed body made him gag when the handkerchief covering his nose and mouth was ineffective. He climbed up on the platform base of the well, peered down into the deep reservoir and noticed the soles of Professor Collins' rubber boots visible just below the water level. He rushed back to the cruiser and called the county coroner over the car's radio, instructing him to get there lickety split. It was a pretty gruesome sight watching them drop that hook, that was often used to recover drowning victims from the bottom of a pond or lake, and pull Professor Collins' carcass to the top of the well. Fortunately, Professor Collins was way beyond the scope of physical pain, so there was a small degree of consolation in knowing that fact.

The circumstances surrounding Professor Collins' accidental, drowning, in his own well, remains a mystery to this day. I surmise he must have taken one trip too many into his dungeon of formaldehyde wonderment, got a bit too lightheaded, went to the well for a cool drink of water, looked down into the deep reservoir, got dizzy and fell in. The thing I can't figure out is why on that particular day, of all days, he neglected to close the hinged doors on top of the well once the bucket cleared the opening of the well. He never, ever left them open. All I can imagine is that he must have had a lot on his mind. And then, too, it just may not have been his lucky day.

On that following Sunday, Sam and I decided to hold a short memorial service for Professor Collins. Mrs. Collins was touched by our act of kindness. We invited all of our neighbors to join us in singing the songs we thought were so appropriate for Professor Collins' untimely demise and character.

Sam sat on the long bench on the right side of the house, gently laid the guitar on his lap, and secured the steel slide over the guitar's neck. Thank goodness for his left-handed habit, and the good fortune that the missing right pinkie would not compromise his musical abilities. When he leaned over to start strumming the first notes, the charm at the end of the thin strand of rawhide around his neck came into view. He casually tucked the white-gold overlaying a yellow-gold base ring back into his shirt, and glanced up at me. We both simply smiled when our eyes met.

Junior Carter had agreed to accompany us with his harmonica in the high-spirited services, and the singing began with the riveting "Wade in the Water" and sailed on with "We Shall Overcome" "Throw Out the Life-line" There's A Great Day Coming" and "Go Down, Moses."

The send off we gave Professor Collins that day was much more than he deserved, but, that was the very least we could do, considering. And I do mean the very least.

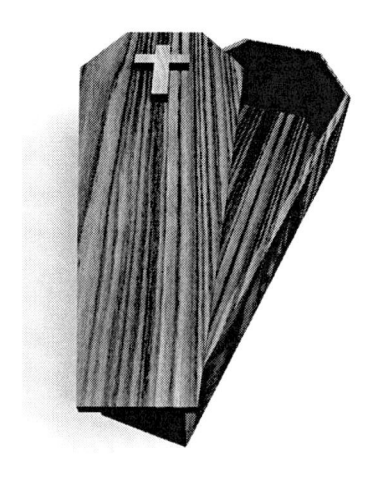

THE SETTIN' UP
(An Old-Fashioned Country Wake)

I remember the day PaPa Willis died. It was on a Tuesday, the 2nd day of September, three days after his 69th birthday.

We'd been at the tobacco barn, and the strip house since the sun came up, and didn't leave 'til it was near set, trying to get all the priming and stripping done in time to get the tobacco to the warehouse for the big auction.

PaPa Willis had been feeling poorly for more than two years and took a turn for the worst about three months before he died. The last week of his life, he went into a coma and never woke up again.

Grammy Willis was a big, robust woman with graying temples, six feet tall, weighing nearly 200 pounds. She was always talkin' 'bout the day them Angels come to, 'Carry Us Home'. When his health couldn't get much worse, she started making plans for PaPa Willis' trip Home.

PaPa Willis worked the coal mines in Casper County for many years. Sometimes, he'd be gone for weeks on end before he'd come home. But Grammy Willis never complained, 'cause, as she put it, 'PaPa Willis was makin' good'. And the money he earned working the coal mines did make what most of the other tenants that sharecropped on Gage Montgomery's farm earned, look pretty skimpy.

He worked sixteen hours most days, and by the end of the week, he'd made a whoppin' $37.75. We felt like we was the richest 'culud' folks in Valencia County. I say 'we' 'cause me and my big brother, Henry Lee, lived under the same roof, although he was on a Navy ship somewhere in the middle of the ocean. It was the only home the two of us had known for more than fourteen years.

Our Momma died before I can remember. And I have no earthly idea where our Pappy is, to this day. Far as I know, or care, he's dead and gone. I never laid eyes on him, not that I can remember. If he walked in here this minute, I wouldn't know him from Adam's apple. In fact, I didn't know none of my Pappy's folks. PaPa and Grammy Willis were my Momma's Ma and Pa, and the only Ma and Pa I ever knew. Grammy Willis said my Pappy ran off, years ago, with some 'high yella' street hussy named Flossie Brown, and hasn't been heard from since. That's why Grammy Willis swore my Momma died of a broken heart.

Grammy Willis called Flossie Brown, 'Wasted Yella', 'cause as she put it, "It's a pure divine sin an' a shame for God to waste light skin on a heffa that ugly." So I say to Pappy and Flossie Brown, "Good riddance!"

Long as I can remember, PaPa Willis had a real bad cough. But I didn't think much of it 'cause most of the men folk 'round here did a lot of nasty harking and coughing. But I got real scared when PaPa Willis started coughing up blood one New Year's Eve. Grammy Willis was worried, too, although, she had a way of never letting it show. I knew she expected the worst.

You see, I'd heard them talking many a times about how bad it was on somebody's lungs to be breathing in all that coal dust. I even remember one or two times when there was a cave in at the mines, and somebody 'got buried alive under tons o' coal', as PaPa Willis put it. They never knew I was listening so I couldn't tell nobody just how worried I was about PaPa Willis. Us young folks knew more than grownups thought we knew. We just didn't let them know we knew. And, the way I figure, I wasn't supposed to know anything about that.

We were supposed to know our place and mind our business, I always been told. So I had no business knowing just how bad off PaPa Willis really was.

The morning before PaPa Willis died, he had a peculiar kind of hazy glow over his face. Old folks called it the 'Death Veil.' He laid there as stiff as a dead door nail, when I tried to feed him his mush and clabber milk, (hominy grits and butter milk) the same breakfast he'd had every morning for as long as I could remember. He called it his 'jump start' breakfast. But he won't having none that day. His teeth were shut tighter than a vice grip when I tried to pry them open with the spoon to feed him. After a while, I just gave up and took the plate back to the kitchen and dumped the food into the slop bucket. *At least the hawgs will enjoy it*, I thought to myself. Of course, Grammy Willis said there was nothing to worry about. But, deep down inside, I did, and so did she.

Each morning, after he no longer got out of bed and spent most of the day sleeping, before I'd go off to who knows where, I would go to PaPa Willis' room and tell him all my plans for the day. Of course, I never did most of what I said I would. It was my way of keeping us connected. Even though I was no longer sure he could hear my voice or understand the words, I continued my morning ritual anyway. And that morning was no different. He didn't even move an eyelash as I rattled on and on. "First thang I'm gon' do, PaPa, is pick me some of them delicious, red apples from that tree on the way to the strip house so I'll have me somethin' to snack on. Then I'm gon' swipe me a few of them blueberries by the side of the path, an' head on my way so we can git the last of dat tobacco to the market an' have some money to go school shoppin'. I already spotted a pair of black and white saddle lace-ups I wanna wear for our school social. I bet you'd like 'em, too. Anyway, I'll see you when I git back, Okay?"

When I was done, I gave him my usual see-you-later kiss, as I always did. But, that time, it was a bit longer than usual. I think, deep down inside, I somehow knew it would be the last.

It had been a beautiful pre-fall day. On the way from the strip house, I made a detour pass T-Bone Wilson's Store just to walk through the grove of oak, maple, and poplar trees that dressed up the crossroads at Old River Lane. And to get a closer look at the winged crop duster as the plane swooped down, releasing a half ton of powdery liquid, which made a loud 'swoosh' noise when the insecticide rained down on the field of cotton.

The fiery red, brilliant yellow, and bronzy brown leaves blanketed the ground below. As I walked along, I made an occasional part between the layers of fallen leaves with the toe of my shoes, leaving a trail behind me. When I glanced upward from my carefree play, I caught a glimpse of Reverend Falcon's blue, 'country Lincoln' (pick-up truck), in front of our white, two-story, wood frame house, just before he pulled off.

My heart fell to my feet; it could only mean one thing, them angels done come to carry PaPa Willis home. He used to joke and say, "When my time comes, I'm gon' put on my 'Broke Iron' shoes an' tap dance through them Pearly Gates shoutin', 'Glory, Halleluiah! I've come home to roost!" Then he'd slap his right knee with the palm of his hand, chuckle and say, "Ahh,

Lawdy!" And settle back in his chair, shaking his head as he let out a big breath, with chewing tobacco spit oozing from the corners of his mouth.

I truly enjoyed all them tall tales PaPa Willis used to tell us. Of course, I knew most of them were lies. We'd be out in the yard playing one of our childish games, holding hands, swinging and swaying from side to side singing, "I dropped the switch. *Where 'bout?* On the ground. *Where 'bout.*" A few minutes later, we'd see PaPa Willis come on the porch and settle down in his old Brentwood rocker. Then he'd yell out, "Come on de porch, chil'ren, PaPa Willis got a story for you."

We'd all gather on the front porch facing him with our legs folded in front of us. We'd watch him cram a big wad of Black Maria Sweet Chewing Tobacco in his jaw before he starts, and prepare ourselves to be well entertained. Every once in a while he'd lean over the arm of the rocker, pick up that empty soup can and shoot a mouthful of spit into the bottom so fast, the story was never interrupted.

He painted such a colorful picture each time he told a new story, we hung onto every word. My favorite story was the one about his friend Herman the Hermit and Jacob Bartholomew Jenkins.

I can hear him now.

"I used tuh have a friend name of Herman Cornelius Henpecker. He went off tuh fight in de big War and when he come back, he was real messed up. Herman didn't like people no mo' 'cause he said, 'I see'd humans do thangs tuh others dat I didn't think no human could do.' So Herman went way down intuh de woods, built hisself a lean-to, and completely shut hisself off from de rest o' de world.

Ah was de only person who evah know'd what happened tuh Herman. Ev'ry once in a while, I'd go deep intuh de woods to check on ol' Herman an' make sho' he was okay. One day when I was gittin' close tuh his camp, I heard growlin' like two animals was 'bout tuh kill each other. When I git tuh de clearin', I see'd t'was ol' Herman 'bout tuh do battle wit' a' 18 foot tall, 4,000 poun' Grizzly Bear, wearin' bibbed ov'ralls and a' ol' top hat.

I see'd dat ol' Grizzly walk up tuh Herman, slap dat grungy fishin' hat off his head, yank on his waist-long, snow-white goatee, an' say, 'I'll jes take dem thar fried catfish off yo' hands if ya don't mind'.

Ol' Herman raised his head way up in de air, looked dat Grizzly Bear in de face, an' said, 'I most certainly does min', thank ya very much'.

Den dat Grizzly bear swatted ol' Herman on his left shoulder wit' his ten-inch claws. Ol' Herman fell back, grabbed his shoulder, an' hollered, 'Good Law, Almighty! Gimme strength!' Den dat bear slapped Herman so hard, he flew 28 foot in de air, slammed intuh a 479 foot tall, 12,875 year old live oak tree, an' slid down tuh de ground.

W'en Herman come up, he was turnin' intuh de Devil. Fangs was growin' out de corners o' his mouth. His ears got pointy like a Wolf, an' a 6 inch horn was growin' out each side o' his head. I said, 'Lawd, hammercy, sweet Moses, who parted de Red Sea, Herman fittin' tuh kill dat thar bear.'

He walked o'er tuh dat bear and punched him in de nose hard as he could. 'Cause ya know a bear's nose is real sensitive, an' when ya hits a bear in de nose, he temp'rarily stunned.

Fo' dat bear kin git hisself together, ol' Herman give him a right hook up side de head, an' another, an' another. Den he swung his left arm way b'hind his back and give dat bear a left uppercut. Knocked dat bear so far in de air, when he come down an' hit de groun', he dug a hole 12-foot deep an' 19-foot wide.

Ol' Herman jumped on dat bear like he was ridin' a horse. He punched him on de right side o' de head, an' de left side o' de head. An' de right side ag'in, 'til dat bear started hollerin,' 'Uncle! Uncle! I give up. You win. You's a better man than me.'

Ol' Herman jumped off dat bear's back, looked him straight in de face, an' said, 'I's a good-hearted man, Jacob Bartholomew Jenkins, ya catfish thief. I hates a thief more'n anythang in de world, Jacob Bartholomew Jenkins, ya catfish thief. If ya wanted some o' these here fried catfish fish, all ya had tuh do was ask, Jacob Bartholomew Jenkins, ya low-down, dirty, snifflin' catfish thief. Now git up an' shake yo'self off.'

'Yessuh, Mr. Herman. Thank ya, Suh. Thank ya.'

Ol' Herman walked o'er tuh dat bear, nose tuh nose, an' said, 'De next time ya comes tuh my camp, an' I done fried me up a big mess o' catfish, I'll welcome ya tuh share 'em wit' me. Do you understand?'

'Yessuh, Mr. Herman. Yessuh. I thanks ya, Mr. Herman. I thanks ya."

'Now turn yo' sorry self 'roun' and drag yo' mangy hide back intuh de brush whar ya com' from.'

Den dat bear tucked his short tail 'tween his legs, dropped his head wit' shame, an' walked back intuh de woods.

I come back home smilin' all de way, knowin' dat ol' Herman gon' be alright. 'Cause if he kin whomp a' 18-foot tall, 4,000 poun' Grizzly bear, he kin whomp anythang.

The next time I come out tuh check on ol' Herman, he an' dat Grizzly bear be sittin' on a log, eatin' a mess o' fried catfish, swappin' lies, an' passin' 'roun' a jug o' Elderberry wine."

PaPa Willis starts laughing, leans back in the rocker, raises his right hand, and swears, *"Hope tuh die. I wouldn't lie."* Then he slaps his right knee and say, *"Ahh, Lawdy!"*

Now I know PaPa Willis well enough to know that when he says, "Hope tuh die. I wouldn't lie," he done told a whopper.

He used to tell me that, "Humans always git ever'thang backward 'cause de Good Book says we s'posed tuh mourn when we come here an' rejoice when we leaves. An' when I close my eyes for de last time," he grinned and continued, "I want y'all tuh throw de biggest Ho Down dis side de Miss'ippi." And that's just what we did.

When I stepped into the back porch, Grammy Willis met me at the door. "Yo' PaPa's gone, L'il Bit," she said, extending her arms to embrace me. She pulled me close and whispered into my left ear. "Clean yo'self up an' go give yo' PaPa a proper good-bye."

Then she took hold of my shoulders and moved me backwards, just far enough to look into my eyes, and continued with an endearing smile on her face. "Then we gon' give yo' PaPa a proper sendin' off an' throw him a party de size o' St. Louis just like he wanted!"

I agreed, shaking my head as I went to my room to wash eight hours of tobacco dust off my body. I put on my best Sunday dress and shoes and strolled into PaPa Willis' room and gave him a proper so long.'

"I'm sure gon' miss you, PaPa. I'm so jealous of all them Angels up there in Heaven that's gon' be keepin' company wit' you, I can't hardly stand it. But you taught me not to be selfish. I had you fifteen years. I guess that's enough to git me through the worst kind of days. But I may have to call on you for help, from time to time, when thangs git a lil too tough for me to handle down here on my own. I know you'll reach down from Heaven an' tap me on the shoulder to let me know you got my back. So go ahead, rest in peace, an' have yo'self a ball hangin' out wit' God, up there in Heaven. I'm gon' be alright."

After I changed again into my regular clothes, I donned one of Grammy Willis' aprons and filled the wash pan with warm water and sat it on the chest of board in his room. Then I gathered a towel, a wash cloth and a fresh bar of lie soap, and we gave him the longest bath of his entire life.

Grammy Willis had tied an old pillow case over his midsection, like a diaper, before I re-entered the room, to protect his dignity.

PaPa Willis won't too keen on taking no baths, except on Saturday nights, to make sure he was good and clean for Sunday church services. He used to say, "Cleanliness is next tuh Godliness only if ya in de House o' de Lawd."

Halfway through the bath, I imagined him cussin' up a white tornado the way we were scrubbing him from head to toe, and on a weekday, to boot. I got so tickled, I fell over on the wash table and send the wash pan crashing to the floor. Soapy water splashed everywhere. Grammy Willis laughed, too, when I told her what tickled me so. She agreed, "He's probably pitching quite a fit on his way through dem 'Pearly Gates'."

"I kin just hear him now, L'il Bit." *'Lawd! take me as I is, 'cause these two females don' washed away all my sanctified soul and scrubbed ev'ry last ounce of religion from dis tired, ol' body.'*

We both had to laugh again.

When we were done with his bath, we dressed PaPa Willis in his best, and only, blue linen suit and tie. We called it his Uncle Sam tie because it looked like the American flag, with red, white, and blue stars and stripes. We gave him a good shaving, combed his salt and pepper hair, and sat his wide-brimmed, Sunday hat midway his head to top it all off. Now he was ready for company.

Grammy Willis and I spent most of the night preparing a feast fit for a king, with fried chicken (fresh off the yard), turnip greens (fresh from the turnip patch), candied yams, corn bread, string beans and potatoes, pineapple, chocolate, and angel food cakes, sweet potato, coconut, and pecan pies, and homemade rolls so light, they'd melt in your mouth.

Every so often, I'd go into PaPa Willis' room and marvel at the handsome, but idly still body stretched across the length of the iron spindled bed, decked in his finest attire, and I'd brag boastfully, "You was the best, PaPa. Folks'll be talkin' 'bout this for months. I can just hear 'em now. *'He sho' was put away good. Best lookin' corpse I evah did see. Somebody sho' did a heck of a job dressin' him for de Hereafter. Got him lookin' better'n most folks still walkin' 'roun' live'."* I had to chuckle, holding my hand over my mouth. I half expected him to sit up and take a bow, 'cause he was quite the show man, and sporty, to boot. Nobody could hold a candle to him when he strolled down the lane with a little swagger in his step, wearing his blue, double-breasted suit. He was a sight to behold. Even as he laid there with his hands folded over his chest, wearing the most peaceful smile I ever did see. And I felt good. He'd suffered long and hard. But the pain was finally gone, and he never once complained; a gentleman never complains. And PaPa Willis was a gentleman amongst all gentlemen.

My trance was broken when Grammy Willis called me back to the kitchen. It was close to 5:00 a.m. before we gave that old wood stove a rest. Grammy Willis and I got about three hours of sleep before neighbors started coming from near and far to pay their last respects. And none came empty handed. Before the day was over, we had enough food to feed a small army.

Peace finally settled over the house around 3:00 p.m. That gave us a couple of hours before the next swarm of well wishers and the procession for the 'Settin' Up.'

Grammy Willis had dressed the floor-to-ceiling windows, in PaPa Willis' room in fine, pale blue, satin drapes she ordered from the Sears and Roebuck catalog when PaPa Willis first started working the coal mines. She covered the bed with a snow-white chenille bedspread. The feather pillows were adorned with white, eyelet pillow cases. I imagined PaPa Willis asleep in a bed of Heavenly Manna.

Since PaPa Willis prided himself on having the best looking flower garden in the county, Grammy Willis filled the room with an assortment of his favorites: red, gold, and burgundy asters, giant yellow mums, and blue hydrangeas. It looked like the president himself was being laid to rest.

THE SETTIN' UP

The huge barn, where we always held the big Ho Down at the end of tobacco season, was decorated with red, white and blue banners, 'cause PaPa Willis was a true American patriot. He fought in the First World War and was all too proud of it. Although, I heard him say too many times, how badly most 'culud' soldiers were treated in those days. He used to say, *"De enemy treated us like dawgs and so did de allies. We was good 'nough tuh fight on de front lines, but not good 'nough tuh eat at de same table. We ate our grub on de back po'ch wit' de strays."*

A half dozen rectangular tables, set in two rows of three each, end to end, also dressed in red, white, and blue stars and stripes, looked like it was the 4th of July. Each one held enough bowls and platters of every kind of food you could think of to make sure that everybody left with a full belly.

The next crowd started congregating just before sundown. Some came on foot, some on horseback, and some on the backs of loaded down pickup trucks, all dressed in their best Sunday-go-to-meeting clothes. The women flaunted their best hats and dresses, the men paraded in their best suits and ties, and they all looked some kinda good; and they knew it.

Sammy Jones was strutting 'roun' like a spring chicken in his grey, pinstripe suit. Johnny Brown thought he was the *cat's meow* in his Stetson hat, and I knew I was the best looking thing in the whole crowd, sporting my black, fishtail dress, that was hugging my waist and hips like a new pair of gloves.

Each wave of visitors respectfully proceeded to the receiving room for one last glance of the decorated veteran they all held in such high regard.

Josh Wilson and Emmett Johnson volunteered to be the official sitters for the body and positioned themselves on either side of the bed as safety nets. That way, if the body experienced any mobilized reflexes as rigormortis completed its process that could cause it to sit straight up in the bed, Josh and

Emmett would be there to catch it before it toppled to the floor. That was the official 'Settin' Up'.

I overheard one admirer remark as he stood by the bed, hands folded at the waist, "He didn't know a man he didn't like." Another added, "He didn't know how tuh say, 'No', no matter how big de favor." And then there was a moment of silence.

The men had all removed their hats as a show of respect and replaced them at the same time as they exited the bedroom. Then they made their way to the front door, across the long porch, and headed down the path to the barn.

Three sides of the barn, facing the East, South, and West, had the tin roof extending an extra 30 feet over the sides; perfect shelter from the pouring rain or the scorching heat, which had all but set in the western sky. A cool, late-summer breeze stirred, causing the table covers to flutter against its gentle caress. The lit kerosene torches, staked around the barn, danced with each fleeting gust. It was a perfect party setting, however deceptive in appearance, which began as a quiet evening of remembrance, and evolved into an untamed soiree of merriment.

I can still hear the rousing R&B serenades carried by the gusting winds, echoing throughout the locality, as Bobby Johnson cranked up the old piccolo and the guests made their way down the path to the barn.

Faster than you could swat a fly off a Blue Tick Hound, we were rocking and rolling to the wailing screams of big Blues legend, Jimmy Reed, spitting out his arousing lyrics to, 'Big Boss Man'.

Before Jimmy could finish serenading the crowd, we were slow-dragging to the satiny voice of, Billie Holiday, singing, 'I'm a Fool to Love You'.

We danced the slop while, Wilbert Harrison swooned us with, 'Going to Kansas City.' The mood toned down with Sam Cooke's smooth melody, 'We're Having a Party'. Needless to say, the mood shifted gears when Sam

THE SETTIN' UP

broke out with the, 'Cha, Cha, Cha'. By the time Lloyd Price got through singing, 'Stagger Lee' and 'Personality,' and Chuck Berry was tired of calling, 'Maybelline,' the energy level shifted into overdrive.

Bobby served up a little island swing when J. T. Thomas appeared from behind the barn, holding a tobacco stick and challenged everybody to 'see how low can you go', and put on the, 'Limbo Rock'. Swoot Jones and E. C. Chavis grabbed hold of each end of the stick and hoisted it up in the air over their heads. One by one, we lowered our shoulders, tilted our heads backwards, and strolled under the stick while the music kept on playing.

I heard J. T. yell out, "Oh, Lawd! My back!" I looked up just in time to see J. R. Evans and Boomer Reavis haul him off to the nearest bench after he went a little too low trying to act like a spring chicken instead of the old rooster he was.

And the music never stopped.

Then the moves and grooves went full throttle when Chubby Checker instructed us to, 'Do The Twist'.

Cousin Jackie Speed strutted into the middle of the crowd and told us to all move back and, "Let me show you how we party in New York City." Then she grabbed hold of her friend, Russell Cross, and asked Bobby to, put on '**The** Harlem Shuffle'. "Me and Russell gon' show 'em how it's done." And Bob and Earl sang out the instructions.

Jackie took two steps forward, and moved her left shoulder back and brushed it with her right hand. Then she slid to the left and to the right, took a dip and came up with her arms extended to the sides, like she was about to take flight. She shimmied up to Russell so close, I thought she was gonna rub the flowers on her dress off on his brown suit. She raised her left hand and kept on shimmying as Bobby flipped the arm on the record player and a new tune started to play. It was Fats Domino singing, 'Blueberry Hill', and 'Walkin' To New Orleans'.

I don't know where the energy was coming from, but the first streaks of dawn were starting to appear in the eastern sky, and we were still struttin' and strollin', windin', grindin', and swingin', when Little Richard started singing, 'Tutti Frutti'. That's just how we were behaving, like a bunch of fruit cakes, who literally, 'Danced the Night Away.'

Around 9:00 a.m. Reverend Falcon returned, followed by a blue pickup carrying the funeral coffin, and the longest pink Cadillac I ever did see. The two undertakers stepped out of the vehicle, went around to the back and lowered the lift gate. They slid the casket to the edge of the gate, hoisted it up on their shoulders, and followed the Reverend.

Eight portly women, dressed in burgundy floor length choir robes, emerged from the car and followed them inside to PaPa Willis' room. The men placed the rectangular box on the floor and left. The women circled the bed and stood quietly waiting for their cue to commence singing. The exhausted partygoers remained on site, waiting to escort PaPa Willis to his final resting place.

Reverend Falcon stepped forward, made a sweeping motion with his right hand, and announced, "Friends, I'd like to introduce The Senior Women's Choir of the First United Methodist Holiness Church of Faith, Hope, and Charity."

He nodded to the choir, and they started singing, "Nearer My God."

Halfway through the song the pallbearers, Bobby, Emmett, Josh, and Russell, began to wrap PaPa in the spread that he was stretched out on, and prepared to lift him from the bed, unintentionally interrupting PaPa Willis' rest. The disturbance caused both of his arms to fall to his side, and the once motionless body, sat straight up in the bed. Relatives and friends scattered like roaches when the lights come on, including me. I headed for the back door, but stopped just on the other side of the bedroom and grabbed hold of the door facing. Grammy Willis stood behind me, holding my shoulders as tight as I was holding the doorframe. I clearly felt the pain of her grip. It seems that PaPa Willis gave a whole new meaning to the phrase, 'Settin' Up.'

I peeped around the door and saw PaPa's head drop to his chest. His hat rolled forward into his lap, and his bottom lip drooped downward, but his eyes never opened. If they had, I would have been halfway across the corn field, before you could shake a stick at a black snake.

The only men left in the room were Reverend Falcon and Emmett, who had taken off running just like the rest of us. But for some reason they both froze in their tracks and rushed back to the bed and caught PaPa just short of him hitting the floor.

Reverend Falcon had dropped his Bible in PaPa's lap when he reached to help Emmett catch the body. Together the men repositioned PaPa on the bed, took a deep breath, and wiped the sweat from their brows. They did what they had to do, but I believe they had the devil scared out of them just like the rest of us.

Reverend Falcon looked at Emmett and said, "Let's go ahead and finish wrapping him before we call the others back." Emmett nodded and Grammy Willis asked, "Kin I help?" The men politely said, "No, Ma'am. We got it." And that time they succeeded in wrapping PaPa in the spread, putting him in the coffin, and nailing it shut, with the help of Josh, Bobby, and Russell, that is, after they got the nerve to return to the room. Through all of this, I'm still clinging to the door, keeping a safe distance from the bed.

The choir came back as far as the back porch and waited for the funeral procession to exit the house.

The four men lifted the coffin from the floor, balanced it on their shoulders, and the funeral procession began. Reverend Falcon stepped in front of the four, statuesque pallbearers, raised his hands when he stepped outside the back porch, and The Women's Senior Choir of the United Methodist Holiness Church of Faith, Hope, and Charity started singing and humming the words to the song that PaPa Willis had written just for his own funeral.

Reverend Falcon led the procession across the yard towards the grave that had been dug earlier that morning, followed by the four pallbearers, the choir, and the partygoers. The choir started singing . . .

De Uppah Side

"Halleluiah! Halleluiah! Halleluiah!
Greet me on de uppah side
Halleluiah! Halleluiah! Halleluiah!
Greet me on de uppah side

I'm 'bout tuh clear dat mountaintop
I serv'd Ya, Lawd, wit' pride
I heard Ya' call my name out loud
So greet me on de uppah side

Halleluiah!
Can't wait tuh shake Yo' hand
Halleluiah!
I'm just a simple man
Halleluiah!
Take me as I am
An' greet me on de uppah side

Halleluiah!
I'm gonna walk wit' Ya
Halleluiah!
I'm gonna talk wit' Ya
Halleluiah!
Sing an' shout wit' Ya
So greet me on de uppah side . . ."

THE SETTIN' UP

As the choir and partygoers positioned themselves on the opposite side of the grave, facing the Reverend, he slowly lowered his hands, prompting the choir to lower their voices. Reverend Falcon delivered the eulogy and the choir continued to sing softly in the background . . .

"Lawd, we's gathered here today," Reverend Falcon began.

"Halleluiah!" the choir sang.

"Tuh deliver de soul o' our dear brother, Willis."

"Halleluiah!"

"He served his purpose, Lawd."

"Halleluiah!"

"He fought a mighty battle down here on Earth."

"Greet me on de uppah side."

"Now, Our Heavenly Father, he's comin' home tuh Ya."

"Halleluiah!"

"We ask Ya tuh welcome him intuh Yo' Heavenly Palace, Dear Lawd."

"Halleluiah!"

"Let him drink de sweet waters served at Yo Table o' Bounty"

"Halleluiah!"

"An' wrap him in de bosom o' Yo' Everlastin' Love."

"Greet me on De Uppah Side!"

The Reverend bent down, picked up a handful of red soil and said, . . .

"Halleluiah!"

"Earth to Earth,"

"Halleluiah!"

"Ashes to Ashes,"

"Halleluiah!"

"Dust to Dust," and he dropped a tiny bit of dirt onto the top of the coffin after each phase, then he concluded with, "AMEN!" Just as the choir sang the last words of the hymn, *"So greet me on de uppah side."*

The reverend held his Bible to his chest, walked over to Grammy Willis and me, shook our hands, and walked quietly towards the back door. All of the partygoers, the choir and Grammy Willis followed.

When the four pallbearers lowered the coffin into the grave, and started shoveling scoops of red clay over the rectangular box, I walked up to the grave and released the single yellow rose I'd been clutching in my hand. I blew a kiss into the six foot hole, and bid PaPa Willis to, "Please Rest in Peace."

When I turned to walk back toward the house, something over head caught my attention, and I looked up just in time to catch sight of a beautiful, snowy white dove, flying straight up into the clouds. It turned and looked down at me and suddenly, right before my eyes, it was PaPa, all decked out in his blue linen suit, Uncle Sam tie, and his Broke-Iron shoes, wearing his trademark big eagle grin. He winked at me and I read that look loud and clear. I started smiling and yelled out to the top of my lungs, "Sail on, PaPa, sail on. You just had to have that one last laugh, didn't you! Pullin' that stunt, sittin' straight up in the bed like that made yo' home-goin' party a pure divine, true *'settin' up'*. I suspect there's gon' be a few less demons walkin' 'round these here parts. Scared the pure livin' hell outta everyone of us."

In a sweet breath, Papa turned into a misty cloud, floated upward and disappeared.

Made me feel so good, next thing I knew, I was hopping on one foot shouting, "AHH, LAWDY, AHH, LAWDY!"

Yea, I guess you could say it was a 'Settin Up' to beat all 'Settin Ups'. And, today, when I get the urge to take one of my ritual strolls down R&B memory lane with **Jimmy, Billie, Wilbert, Sam, Chuck, Chubby, Lloyd,**

Bob, **Earl, Fats**, and **Little Richard**, it warms my heart to know that PaPa Willis is up there on the other side of them Pearly Gates. Sharing one of his tall tales, dancing a jig in his gold-trimmed, Broke-Iron Shoes, keeping a watchful eye on his wayward flock down here on the low end of God and thanking the Lawd for letting him have one last 'settin' up'. Makes me feel so good, I just gotta say it one more time, *"AHH, LAWDY! GREAT DAY IN THE MORNIN'!"*

POETRY

GRE'T DAY 'N DE MORNIN'!!

The durndest thang I ever see'd
Two big, black bruthas
Fightin' like fools on hands an' knees
One holler's "you mutha f----!
I throwed dat durned seven"
The uthah one hollered, "You black sucka!
You kno' you throwed a 'leven!"

Knock-down-drag-out Saturday night fights
'roun these here parts
they's a common sight.
Whiskey-drinkin, crap-shootin' sons-of-guns
gamble all night long
way into Sunday morn.

Ol' one-eye Johnny Tate was de ace
o' Black Jack Hill.
Got dat right eye knocked
o'er a five dollar bill.
Shootin' craps one Saturday night
wit' Pa an' red-eyed Jody Gill.
Under dat washed out foot bridge
on de other side o' Peter Gill Hill.

De Saturday night fights was never complete
'til Pinto Brown come 'roun'
startin' fights wit' ev'rybody he see'd.
One time, see'd him choke a po
wino half to death.
Wrapped dem big, black hands 'roun '
dat po fella's neck
an' squeezed 'til he pee'd all o'er hisself

Used to come 'roun' our back door
winkin' dem big, red eyes at me.
I ain't never tell Ma 'bout dem ten-dollar bills
He used to offer me for some o' my 'CANDY'.
I cussed him out an' pat my a— in his face
D'en I sick dat ol' hound dawg on him
An' he chased his ashy a— all o'er de place.

Lookin' back on dem jumpin'-good times
t'was GREAT DAYS EV'RY MORNIN'
ev'ry day o' de week.
In de afternoon, the evenin'
the midnight hour, an' in between,
LIFE WAS FINE, DANDY AN' ALL OUT SWELL.
Back there in dem good ol' foot-stompin' days,
Us countrified, culud folks raised all kinds o' Hell!

GUNNY SACKIN'

"Don't you tell Massa
We gon' steal dis corn
Snuck up here from de cotton patch
W'en we see'd him leave home

We take off dese shucks
He'n gon' know no diff'rence
He thinks dat ol' mare
Done broke pasture ag'in

Now shuck it fast; we'n got much time
Massa catches us in dis here co'n field
He gon' whip our 'hinds
An' make us pick cotton
An' won't give us nary dime!

You know our Mammy don't take to no slavin'
Us pickin' cotton for nothin'
'Cause we been misb'havin'

So fill dis ol' gunny sac
An' throw it o'er my back
An' let's git de devil outta dis here co'n field
'Fo Massa gits back!"

Mary Noble Jones,

The tranquil country setting depicted in this picture is the work of artist and author, Mary Noble Jones. She is a native of Amelia, Virginia and the author of the children's book series, The Adventures of Itzy & Wiggles. In 2008 she published her novel **Childhood Memories** and in 2010 her latest novel, **Secrets & Skeletons**. For more information on her works please visit her website at:
www.marynoblejones.com.

The Author

G. P. Marrow

G. P. Marrow is the youngest of eight children, born to share-croppers, Martha Ann Carroll-Marrow and Walter Marrow, outside the small, piedmont, North Carolina town of Henderson, in Vance County.

She has been an aspiring writing since the age of eight, and attributes her love for reading and writing to her mother, who, herself, had a unique talent for story-telling.

Ms. Marrow has an Associate Degree in *Secretarial Science*. In 2009, she earned an Associate of Applied Science Degree in Early Childhood Education/Teacher Associate from Vance-Granville Community College in Henderson, North Carolina.

Great Day In The Mornin': Country Folks Cuttin' Up,. her first book of short stories, published by Black Deer Books, is currently available through bookstores, and on the internet.

Please visit Ms. Marrow at her website at:
www. gpmarrow.com
and she would love to receive your email at:
GPMarrow@aol.com